Gina Davidson writes by default. She went to art school and music college under the misguided impressions that she was a) artistic and b) musical, then to teachers' training college in a desperate bid to qualify herself for adult life. Dogged by boredom, she perceived herself as a late developer and went to London University as a mature student where she gained an MA in eighteenth-century English. Her attempts at short story writing and journalism have been acclaimed for their dark humour and eccentric charm and her reflections on motherhood are recorded weekly in the pages of the *Guardian*. She lives in North London with her teenaged daughter and a boxer bitch called Poppy.

TREASURE

The TRIALS OF A TEENAGE TERROR

GINA DAVIDSON

A *Virago* Book

First published in Great Britain by VIRAGO PRESS 1993

Reprinted 1993, 1994 (twice), 1995 (three times), 1996

A CIP catalogue record for this book
is available from the British Library.

ISBN 185381 711 2

Printed in England by Clays Ltd, St Ives plc

Virago
A Division of
Little, Brown and Company (UK)
Brettenham House
Lancaster Place
London WC2E 7EN

To my special treasure, Amy,
and to Grandma and Grandpa, with love

Contents

The telephone   1

Treasure goes to the cinema   4

The night club   8

Treasure is not appreciated   11

Spring at our house   14

Treasure's pocket money   17

The girls next door   20

The perfect boy   22

Treasure's night out   25

Treasure and the perfect boy   28

Treasure does her homework   30

Feeding Treasure   33

The Wonderbra   36

Treasure visits her grandparents   38

Treasure on holiday   41

Summer   47

Treasure's inherited temperament   49

Grandma's food supplies   51

Treasure and the neighbours   53

Treasure and the critics   56

Grown-ups behaving badly   59

Treasure the lifesaver 62

Saving the dinner 65

Treasure's attitude to clothing 67

The goldfish murderer 70

Treasure's best friend 73

Treasure tidies up 76

Grandpa's tidying 79

Treasure the hostess 80

Nightmare on Oxford Street 83

Beginning of the clothes problem 86

The two faces of Treasure 90

Treasure changes her mind 93

Treasure talks of boyfriends 96

Treasure asks too much 99

Treasure's good report 102

Winter 105

Treasure's seasonal dilemma 107

Treasure the romantic 110

A dangerous evening 113

Treasure takes a bath 116

The telephone. Part 2 119

Treasure the rebel 122

The blue room 125

Treasure helps with the decorating 128

The dog at table 131

The telephone. Part 3   133

Treasure and the generation gap   136

Terrifying shopping   139

Treasure the supervisor   141

An almost pleasant morning for us   145

Treasure's high standards   148

Treasure's bicycle   151

Passing the dog test   154

The comparative behaviour of boys   156

Bargain or blackmail?   159

Treasure goes to the party   163

Treasure's footwear   165

The saintly side of Treasure   168

Lodger's departure   171

Treasure's school uniform   174

Watching television   177

School rules   180

Our outing   183

The several ages of Treasure   186

Holiday plans   190

Ruder and ruder clothing   192

Hereditary anxiety   194

Treasure's timetable   199

Treasure and the feminine mystique   202

The cultured side of Treasure   207

The telephone

It is spring and all along our street the teenagers are running amok. In the light evenings and through the open windows they can be seen and heard shrieking, skulking, turning to sex, drugs, 18-plus videos and undesirable friends, kicking footballs about and setting off the car alarms. An upmarket brand of youth can sometimes be seen lolling against the front garden walls employing a cordless telephone.

In our house the telephone rings relentlessly. Treasure's life has opened out on the end of it. She can Go Out with people by telephone and she can Dump Them. She can have whole relationships without any physical contact. Once on it she loses track of time, even peak time. It flies by at 38p a minute.

I've tried limiting her telephoning – between eight and nine was to be Treasure's phoning time, otherwise – and this is the ultimate threat – I will be rude to them.

'I hate you,' shrieks the Treasure. 'Nobody else's mother is so nasty and spiteful.' She is already deeply ashamed of me. 'Everybody knows I've got a mother with red glasses who swears,' she weeps. 'I hate you.'

She hasn't quite understood my instructions, assuming not that she *may* use the phone between eight and nine, but that she *must*. On the dot of eight she springs to it and phones like billy ho. Eager for calls, she snatches up the receiver mid-first-ring. Should I use the phone even briefly during *her* time, say to ask my neighbour for a carrot, Treasure is incensed. 'This is MY time,' she bellows.

Then one night at ten thirty the phone rings. (As it is the weekend there is no such thing as bedtime.) Treasure snatches it up. 'Hallo. What? Hallo?' Pause. 'Hallo?' She puts it down and returns to the sofa ashen and silent.

'What's the matter?'

'Nothing.' Treasure has gone almost green.

'What is it?'

Her face begins to crumple. It was Lizzie from down the road. An abusive phone call. 'You bitch. What have you said about me? You cow. I hate you, I hate you.'

The story unfolds. So-and-so told so-and-so, who told the whole school, that Treasure said Lizzie was a lesbian, but she didn't really, honestly she swears she didn't, and anyway Lizzie had phoned up Treasure's friends and told them she was a liar and to write her horrid letters.

'She's been ringing all my friends and telling them to say nasty things to me because I haven't spoken to her since she said I could go the cinema and then I went over there and she said "Go away, you can't come because Samantha's coming." '

'I don't deserve this,' screams the Treasure, top

volume. 'What have I done to deserve this?' She beats the sofa with her fists. She is beside herself, poisoned by the telephone. Will this cure her? No. She's back on it at dawn, phoning M to find out what he said to R and phoning L to tell all, and so a great relay of phoning begins.

I go out to Sainsburys. The previous evening was ruined and this morning the house is tense and the telephone clogged by Treasure's drama. I return to find Treasure, Lizzie and two neighbouring boys playing tennis in the road and shrieking happily. They are all friends.

'All girls are like this,' says my neighbour Mrs Perez. Hers are now twenty and twenty-one and living elsewhere. Boys are apparently different, more curt. I spoke to one that afternoon by telephone while the house was empty.

'Is your mother in?'

'No.'

'Could you please tell her I phoned?'

'Erp.'

'Goodbye.'

'Erp.'

I never wanted a son before.

Treasure goes to the cinema

Treasure's friend Lizzie calls by unexpectedly. Would Treasure like to go to the cinema? Yes. Treasure has for once done her homework and is only gawping at the television and intermittently pecking at her Gameboy. The cinema would just be a larger square for her to look at, plus ten minutes' fresh air en route.

Off they go down the road. I've forgotten to ask which film they're going to see and where. I run after them. I have no shoes on. 'Where are you going?'

'Holloway Road.'

'The Odeon?'

'No. The other one.'

Too late I realise there is no 'other one'. They are fast disappearing down the road, my front door is open, the dog will get out, robbers will get in, my feet are cold. 'Which cinema? Which film? When does it end?' I am screaming down the road.

I run back into the house. It is dark, I don't know where the Treasure is going, I am a negligent mother and the whole street knows. Why did I allow her to leave the house in such a casual way? Quickly, out into the car to track them down and ask all the questions I should have asked in the first place. There they are, disappearing round a dark corner on the way to no known cinema.

I follow slowly, sidelights on only. Where are the little toads going? They stop and loiter aimlessly. I call from my car window. 'Where are you going?'

Treasure is mortified. 'It's my mother,' she splutters. 'My mother is following us in the car. Can you believe this?'

A boy has joined them, intensifying Treasure's shame. Two peers have now witnessed her hideous mother creeping along spying on her from a car.

'My mother is following me.' Treasure repeats the phrase as if repetition will force her to accept the appalling truth. She gapes at me, horrified, her friends sniggering in the background.

'Will you leave me alone,' she rasps. 'Just go away. I can't believe this.' She rolls her eyes at her friends and all sneer in unison.

'Just tell me what film you're going to see and at what cinema and I'll go home.' I feel I have made a reasonable request.

'I don't KNOW.' Treasure is enraged. She has been asked a question of immense stupidity. She isn't ashamed in the least that she has been caught fibbing on the way to no cinema.

'The Cannon,' says Lizzie, 'to see *Curly Sue*.'

Treasure is speechless. She has never experienced such humiliation. 'Just go away,' she snaps, sizzling with hatred.

I drive home weeping and phone Lizzie's mother. I

have never spoken to her before and expect a calm, liberal mama who knows her daughter's whereabouts and would never dream of spying and trailing about in a car. But no! This woman is in despair. She pours out her soul, the floodgates open. She is thrilled at the sound of another ineffectual and hated mother. She had assumed the title of most hideous mother in London, and here am I claiming it for myself. No, she has no idea of her daughter's plans, whereabouts, who she's meeting or when she's coming home. She has no control, has lost her grip. She too is sneered, smirked, hissed and sworn at. And the lies. The endless lies.

My heart warms instantly to this woman. We form a pact. We will report all known plans and cross-check all stories to flush out the inaccuracies – a pincer attack on the two of them.

Just then the front door bursts open – a dramatic entrance by Treasure. I quickly put down the phone as she stamps into my room, purple with rage.

'How dare you follow me? I hate you. I was so embarrassed I had to come home. I ran all the way and I'm going to Jane's. I'm not staying here.' Slam. Off she whirls to the youthful neighbour of twenty-six with whom she feels a rapport and to whom she can rant freely about her wicked old bat of a mother. I quickly ring Lizzie's mother with a report – name of cinema, film and reassurances – but what a relief that my own Treasure, however obnoxious, is safely home.

She returns shortly and flings herself on to the sofa, sabotaging the TV news. Strangely her mood seems to have mellowed slightly. She requests hot chocolate, choc-chip biscuits, two bananas and an apple and then confesses all. Her friends were not going to the cinema. They were going to the Heath in the dark to smoke cigarettes. Knowing about the Heath's resident deranged tramp and the odd rape, murder and crucifixion that have occurred up there, Treasure chickened out, blaming her horrid mother, for whom she now expresses a smidgin of affection.

But it won't last. This is only a temporary reprieve. The average teenager on the road to independence often tramples adults underfoot. And we still have exams, sex, drugs, cars and motorbikes to come.

The night club

Treasure's outings are becoming more and more hazardous. She has chummed up with some fifteen-year-olds
who look like eighteen-year-olds and can enter adult
night clubs. Treasure is planning to go to the Strobe Club
tomorrow to hear Indie music, beginning at ten thirty
and ending somewhere near dawn.

The Strobe Club is up by the tube station, guarded by
Sumo-sized bouncers, its darkened doorways crammed
with raggedy, bald and tattooed youth, mainly white-
faced, scowling and dressed in black.

'Can I go tomorrow Mummy? Lizzie, Rosie, Henry
and Sam will call for me at ten on the way there.'

I mention that ten is rather late for the beginning of
an outing and when does she intend coming home? I give
Treasure a stern and determined look. She misinterprets
at once.

'What are you looking at me like that for? You don't
trust me,' she screams hoarsely. Roaring obscenities, she
rushes out slamming the door. She has spoilt my grasp of
8   the plot of *LA Law*. She returns to spoil the news headlines.

'Why can't I go? Everybody else's mother lets them. They can go home at two.' In her fury Treasure has not noticed that I only queried the time of her outing. I didn't ban it altogether. I demand Rosie's mother's telephone number. Treasure slams down her filofax before me, reciting countless numbers as if to the Gestapo. 'Is that enough?' she snaps icily. 'Would you like more?'

Rosie's mother is not the careless figure described by Treasure. She agrees that midnight should be hometime. Fortified by this alliance I inform Treasure that I will meet her outside the Strobe at midnight precisely, with the dog.

'No,' screams Treasure, terrified, wrenching fiercely at my best T-shirt. 'You're *not* coming. Nobody else's mother comes.' She throws herself on to her bed, weeping with shame.

'If this goes on you won't go anywhere.'

'I will,' she shrieks. 'I'll run away. I'll stay out all night.'

She vows to live on the streets. I cancel my Friday night outing in order to be on the spot ready to call the police or personally bust the Strobe. Treasure and I go to bed exhausted.

In the morning I research the Strobe further. Mrs P's daughter, older now and more mature, says it's quite safe. No drugs. Certainly not downstairs where Treasure's going. And the girl from across the road goes there from an apparently well-adjusted and stable family. Daddy's a lecturer, Mummy's a doctor. The Strobe is obviously today's equivalent of the local youth club, safe as the dances I used to go to in my Martini-label skirt.

So Treasure goes in the end, agreeing to all my harsh

conditions. On the dot of midnight she comes bouncing out of the doors. She seems suspiciously cheerful about leaving.

'What was it like?'

'Really nice. They nearly didn't let us in, but we said "Please please," so they did. I thought I might fall down and get trampled,' says she airily, 'but then I saw someone fall down and everybody was very kind and picked them up, so I wasn't worried any more.' Style of dancing seemed to be jumping up and down heavily on the spot, perhaps due to the lack of space. It took Treasure twenty minutes to fight her way to the exit. She chatters on. 'The man next to me was arrested for rolling a spliff. I don't know how they saw him in the dark. I don't think I'm going again to Indie music.'

I am relieved that my Treasure has escaped this pit of hell, this rat-hole, hopefully unscathed. But she had kindly toned down her report for me. I hear her the next day phoning a friend.

'Really good, but everyone's a bit weird. Rosie got a black eye, I got head-butted and Lizzie and Marianne fell down and got trampled on. I'm never going there again with clogs on.'

Her plans for next weekend are rather demure – a Saturday job in a small supermarket and, for relaxation, synchronised swimming.

Treasure is not appreciated

Treasure has a job. She's been after it for weeks. From the moment she saw the new mini-market on the corner she fell in love with it. She pleaded daily with the management to employ her. She took Daisy and doubled the pressure. Management, faced by two potential slaves, took them on.

Treasure comes home thrilled to bits on her first Saturday. She will only take half an hour for lunch, has worked like a demon, refused all offers of snacks and stunned the management with her skills and charm.

'They want me to go on the till,' she prattles during her ten-minute top-speed lunch break. 'I'm too quick, I'm called the Angel and they want me to tutor their children.'

'How much are they paying you?'

'I don't know,' she snaps. 'Just leave me alone.' She rushes off for another four hours of slave labour. This is a heavy weekend. Treasure attended the Strobe Club until midnight on Friday (Daisy's brother had free tickets), is working all today and tonight is off partying in Golders Green. Will I take her to Golders Green in the car? Can she have some money? I am beginning to resent my role as chauffeur and fund-raiser.

'Didn't they pay you?'

'No. I'm late. They'll pay next week. I must have some money for Daisy's birthday present.'

I tell the Treasure that I have hardly any cash. She is incensed. Here she is, forced by poverty to go to work while her mother lolls around teaching. 'Why don't you get a proper job?' she shrieks. 'You never do anything.'

We drive to Golders Green in silence, both sulking. At the appointed place Treasure zooms off to hang out and party, returning obediently at midnight but with four friends. In their presence Treasure and I affect the pose of a pleasant family unit. Treasure wears the mask of an affectionate and obedient child. Gone is the vixen of the afternoon.

'We're very hungry,' says she, ever so civilised. 'May I make everyone some pasta?'

'Make pasta,' say I, sloping off to bed. I don't want to discourage Treasure. She is a hospitable child. It's my own fault. I egged her on in the first place. Years ago her little friends would come round, play with Sindy dolls and Treasure would offer them a biscuit and juice. Her friends are bigger now. They are often tall, hulking and ravenous. They move in packs, arriving at no particular time, but it makes no difference because Treasure no longer observes mealtimes. The whole day is now a potential meal/snacktime. Treasure will empty the larder for her friends in a benevolent way, using up three weeks' Sainsburys supplies in a trice.

I manage to relax, skilfully blocking from my mind

all thoughts of Treasure and her friends in the kitchen: scalding water, boiling oil, lights and grills left on, the house ablaze at dawn and the empty larder. I have hidden my best dark chocs behind the flour. I fall asleep, only to be woken later by Treasure.

'Mummy.' She pushes open my bedroom door. Hundred-watt light blazes in. I feign sleep.

'Mummy.' She is persistent.

'What is it?' I wake up properly and spot the clock. 'It's quarter to bloody three.' My voice has a roaring cracked tone. It rises to primal scream. 'GO TO BED.'

Treasure is shocked by my response. She not only works for a living but has just entertained and cooked for her own friends.

'I only came in to kiss you goodnight,' she whispers. 'I was trying so hard to be good.'

Spring at our house

Treasure has become rather intolerant of the dog. She objects wildly to its dribbling and barking while we eat. She roars cruelly at it, ordering it from the room.

'Get her out of here,' she screams. 'I can't stand it.'

I can understand her revulsion. The dog is not a plus at dinner parties. Bubbles and dribbles dangle and pour from its jowls, forming a slimy puddle on the tiles or carpet beneath. A bark will jerk the slobber so that blobs fly about, sometimes landing on clothing or even on the table. I admit that I have brought the dog up badly. It has now taken to glaring while dribbling, in an accusatory and tragic rather than an aggressive way. It is never satisfied and desires every known food. Recently it has grown to love melon, avocado and kiwi fruit. It cries in a moving way when denied these foods, almost forming vowel sounds. I feel it could be trained to speak. It has a saintly nature and dribbling is its only flaw. I cannot punish it for this natural problem.

Lodger deeply resents my tolerance of the dog's more repulsive habits. I sense that he is jealous. I don't care.

14

The dog has an important role to play in our house. It frightens burglars away and only the other day it helped me to combat vice.

Treasure had the gang around pre-Strobe. They had commandeered the living room during my absence and I returned to find them watching a video nasty with the lights off. I spotted, through the flickering gloom, the outline of couples, intertwined in a romantic way. Quick as a flash I sent the dog in to break them up. If she spots anything erotic going on she likes to join in. She will leap up and kiss the protagonists. She weighs four and a half stone and her kisses are not often welcomed.

An uproar ensued and no more couples. This is probably a good thing. In my youth our headmaster at college warned us about couples.

'A pair is a stultifying unit,' said he strictly. 'Form a gang.'

But Treasure and her friends are not the only ones. Perhaps it is the effects of spring. This morning I hear a strange roaring sound in the garden and a disturbance in the pond. Piles of frogs are having a romantic time out there in the sun. Hordes of them are clutching each other and purring. The dog and I spy on them. Lodger appears and rather taints my pleasure by making tasteless remarks. I order him to leave the garden. Treasure is out on the Heath with her chums missing this unique event in our very own garden. I've heard what this is called on Radio Four. Our frogs are apparently in 'a cluster of sexual frenzy'. Luckily Treasure returns home in time to witness it. I alert her the minute she enters the door.

'Come and look at the frogs. You must see.'

Treasure is blasé. 'Just a minute,' she snaps. 'Who phoned me?'

I relate a mile-long list of names. Treasure must of course phone them before looking at the frogs. She eventually strolls into the garden in a laid-back way. Even she is impressed. She reports to Lizzie on the phone a rather unpleasant version of events.

'Guess what? The frogs are all screwing in our garden. There's so many of them you can't see the water.'

By two o'clock the frogs are resting. They are either exhausted or embarrassed by the vulgar comments made by Lodger and Treasure. I am rather disappointed by the generally crude response to what I regarded as one of the delights of spring. Emulating the frogs, the dog clings to my leg. I am finding it difficult to have feelings of a spiritual or aesthetic nature.

Treasure's pocket money

Treasure was born to spend. She therefore needs huge amounts of pocket money. It is her life blood, she can scarcely move without it. She spends it, lends it, donates it, loses it. She buys snacks, tickets, make-up, bargain offers and presents. She is a fountain of pocket money and I am the source of her wealth – the magic porridge pot. Treasure says the correct words and up comes more pocket money. Because without it she is a prisoner in the house, an unpleasant option for both of us.

'I must have some,' she begs. 'I need it. I had to pay all the taxi fare because no one else had any money. They're all going to pay me back.'

'Good. Then you'll have some money.'

'But I haven't got enough money to *get* to them.' Treasure is at her wits' end. 'You don't understand how much I spend on fares.' She is addressing an ignoramus. 'Fares are very expensive.' Her needs are always pressing. This month has been particularly pressing because it was Peter's birthday and Chloe's birthday *and* she had to buy Easter eggs.

I am keen to know how much pocket money her friends get. Treasure doesn't know. Her friends don't know either. They become confused when asked. They don't even remember whether they have to earn it by doing the odd household task. This is a mysterious grey area.

Treasure is meant to do certain chores to earn her money. She doesn't refuse. She will do them, she promises, but she has other more urgent duties – dancing in her room, hugging the dog, phoning Rosie, going to sleep. In my weak way I have not always enforced these rules. Naturally people have criticised. 'You're making a rod for your own back,' bellows Grandma. She compares her indolent grandchild to the girls who used to live next door. They were paragons in Grandma's eyes. They peeled potatoes, made beds, washed up, never answered back. Having given up on me, Grandma tries Treasure.

'There's only one thing I want you to do,' she begs Treasure in a tragic way. 'Just help your mother. That's all I want you to do.'

This request always throws Treasure into a sullen fury. Grandma's wishes have never been realised. I continue to dole out pocket money regardless. But at least Treasure is a generous child. She spends the bulk of it on presents. I do rather well out of her pocket money. I even have a Teasmade. I have chocs, flowers, tapes and my birthdays are sumptuous affairs. Nevertheless I have cut the pocket money now and then when Treasure's behaviour has gone beyond the pale. But that ploy no longer works. Treasure has a new ally. The bank.

18   The wicked bank tempted Treasure with a cash card

and tons of free gifts. It advertised on TV. All her saved up birthday and Christmas present money can now be frittered with ease. The bank is eager for Treasure to join our nation of debtors and be one of them. It does not wish to encourage thrift. I am no match for such an opponent. I dream that one day, when all Treasure's savings are gone and I am bankrupt, necessity will force me to be strict about pocket money.

Treasure must have read my mind. 'I don't want you to give me all my pocket money,' says she out of the blue. 'I want to save it. I want you to put it in this piggy bank in your room so I can't get it.' She stuffs a fiver into the pig. 'Can I have some advance pocket money? I need three pounds. I must have it.'

'But you've got that five.'

'I can't spend that,' says Treasure. 'I'm saving it.'

The girls next door

Grandma had always been very impressed by the Rodrigo girls next door. 'Those girls know how to behave,' she said, as she sat in the back garden making tiaras out of white convolvulus. She twisted the ropes of it into circles and put it on to Chrissie and Elena's beautiful dark heads, and their long hair, loose, just washed and drying in the sun, looked entrancing. Grandma was surrounded by angels. Treasure, only eight, got a tiara too, but Grandma implied that it wasn't truly deserved.

'All I pray for is that I'll live long enough to see you help your mother,' said she rather dramatically.

Treasure still managed to stay friends with the girls. She missed them terribly when they emigrated. They had been her very best friends for years and played Sindy dolls with her for hours and hours. Their departure was very difficult for everyone.

The girls might have been handy to have around now. Mrs Rodrigo overheard them chatting about sex one day. She would sit by the kitchen window and their voices floated up to her from the garden.

'Erk,' said Chrissie. 'I'm never letting anyone do that to me. I don't care if I can't have babies. I'm never doing *that*.' If Chrissie had retained that view, she might have been a useful influence. At present Treasure expresses no such revulsion. She is keen to rush headlong into relationships with boys. Having a boyfriend is a must, as far as Treasure is concerned.

'Your friend rang up,' I told her the other day. Treasure was immediately infuriated.

'My BOYFRIEND,' she shouted bossily. 'Why can't you say it? Other mothers do. BOYFRIEND.'

I still can't work out exactly what sort of relationship this implies. I was rather baffled last year by the phrase 'going out', before Treasure had a real boyfriend. Mrs B attempted to explain it to me because her daughter had told her, being less ratty and more forthcoming than Treasure. Going Out meant that although you weren't physically Going Out, you couldn't Go Out with anyone else. These partnerships were most serious. I obviously made a big mistake in disregarding them.

The girls next door were never even allowed to contemplate such a thing. They had a Spanish father who kept them under strict supervision. No staying at friends' houses for the night, even ours, no babysitters (so no outings for Mrs Rodrigo either) and they were never allowed to have their hair cut. Mrs Rodrigo had to trim it in secret. I wonder if they've turned out a success.

The perfect boy

Mrs Perez, my neighbour, is ever so proud of her boy. His report has arrived showing him to be perfect. It is crammed with As. He already was something of a paragon. He sings in the choir, does his homework sitting properly at a desk in his room, is never rude and offensive, is pleasant to his mummy and daddy and never stays out late or attends the Strobe. Mrs P is tremendously relieved. She had begun to worry that she too was an inadequate parent, because of her big girls being rather wild in their youth, but now she has produced a pearl.

'How has such a child emerged from the misery of our home?' asks Mrs Perez, stunned by her good fortune. She gazes around her living room, which she feels to be shabby. If she stands in her front bedroom and looks down out of her window, she can see proper families on the other side of the road living in smart homes with south-facing gardens. She sees, now and then, the therapist's husband coming home from Sainsburys, unloading the bags and child from the car; she sees the architects driving off in their jeep for a weekend in Kent.

Four years ago the council planted trees that blossomed white in the spring along both sides of the road. A passerby may never have known the difference but it seemed to Mrs P and myself that on our side the bulk of the residents were in some way faulty. Ours was the side of broken marriages, sulking husbands, struggling, discarded wives, smokers' coughs and leaking roofs – of uncontrollable teenagers and tantrumming smaller children with messy pets.

Between the shady back gardens the walls had crumbled away in parts and in Treasure's childhood cats, rabbits and guinea-pigs ran amok, fouling and devastating the borders. At weekends, holidays and in the late afternoons, children from the seven neighbouring houses would run across the bottoms of the gardens, balancing along the end wall, scrambling over the crumbling parts, backwards and forwards, fighting and playing and wearing down the remaining bits of wall, trampling the ends of lawns.

It was a paradise for children. Treasure loved it – a seven-garden-long safe playground with friends, swings, Tarzan ropes and tadpole ponds always available. But Mrs Perez used to feel that for *her* children, leaving the gardens and coming into the house meant coming into an empty hole in which their mother shuffled about like a husk, somehow just managing to prepare meals and clean clothes.

It was a depression lasting for years. Mrs P feels better now. She has other pleasures. In the mornings while the husband is still asleep or out, she will have her own breakfast: fresh coffee in a delicate china cup (not a mug), warm toast with thick butter and marmalade, sometimes a boiled egg. Sometimes, on lovely summer mornings, I have found her having breakfast in the garden. The lawn is thick and velvety, the lilac chubby and heavily perfumed, the honeysuckle and other shrubs flourishing and the peonies fat and red. Now and then she sleeps there in the afternoons after work on a sunbed, catching the last of the sun, and it is quite as beautiful as over the road. Hers was the last garden of the seven and had always been the least played in. Children would climb over the wall and collect the Perez boy and take him away to the other gardens to swing and play. And now here he was, grown up a success.

Treasure's night out

Treasure is to spend the night at a friend's house. She's been there before, loved it, was quite safe. So I've booked an evening out for myself. It's six o'clock, I've just had a perfumed and relaxing bath, am dressed to leave for the theatre. Treasure telephones. Her voice sounds rather weak.

'Hallo Mum.'

'Are you alright?'

'Yes,' weedily.

'Having a good time?'

'Yes.' Fainter.

'What's the matter? Where's Daisy?'

'She's in her brother's room talking to his friends. I've just come in here to phone.'

Mysterious behaviour from Treasure, who is usually keen to have little to do with her mother when socialising.

'Can't you be in the brother's room? Is something wrong?'

Treasure's voice drops to a whisper. 'They're taking drugs.'

'What sort of drugs?' An unpleasant feeling of cold hackles rising on the back of my neck and shoulders.

'It's called "spliff",' Treasure hisses down the phone.

'It's not dangerous,' say I calmly. 'Just don't have any.'

'Daisy's eyes have gone white and she keeps falling over,' says Treasure, warming to her theme. 'They all keep laughing.'

'Don't worry,' I instruct, sweating quietly. 'When's her mother coming home?'

The mother is expected home in half an hour. I won't cancel the theatre and race to Stoke Newington to rescue Treasure from a junior opium den. The mother will arrive home from work, drugs will be hidden away, Treasure will be safe nestling on the sofa bed in Daisy's room fed on pizza and videos, just as she was last time. Treasure seems relieved. She doesn't really want her mummy to whizz over and scoop her up in the car. She wants to be collected early in the morning, promises to refuse drugs and await the mother.

It had to happen. Thirteen is perhaps rather premature but this is London in the nineties where sex, drugs, Aids, rape, Ecstasy and ruination await the average teenager. Treasure at least reported back the first sign of it. I go out for the evening and attempt to enjoy myself in a carefree way.

At 9 a.m. I arrive to pick the Treasure up. Everyone is asleep. I wake them up by banging on the window. The mother is in attendance. Treasure is smiling pleasantly, everything seems to be in order, until we get into the car. Treasure is apparently an ace thespian. Her smile was false, her calmness masked turmoil. She explodes as we drive off.

26

'Did you smell her mum? The mum smelt. You must have noticed.'

I hadn't noticed. Everything had smelt perfectly respectable to me. But the mum had disgraced herself in all sorts of ways. She'd arrived home at the expected hour, but only to nip into the brother's room and partake of the drugs herself. And worse still, brought home alcohol but no food. No snacks were provided, no fruit, no dinner, not even a scrap of bread for a sandwich. Only drink. Treasure was disgusted and eventually fed on cereal. What's more, reported Treasure, the mother went out again during the evening, returned with a boyfriend and dreadful noises could then be heard coming from the bedroom. My own misdemeanours are now as nought, compared to the transgressions of Daisy's mum – demon of all mothers – lack of snacks rating as the most dire, even worse than drugs, drink, sex and the smell.

Here we have a woman working full time, caring alone for two stroppy teenagers and trying to squeeze some pleasure out of life for herself on a Saturday night. I hate to criticise. And she's done me a favour. I have, in Treasure's eyes, even if only briefly, become a paragon. I am relatively odourless, supply large quantities of food, rarely drink, take no drugs and no rude noises ever come from my bedroom.

Treasure and the perfect boy

Treasure has a strange relationship with the perfect boy. Sometimes she's his friend, sometimes she isn't. The boy does nothing to inspire these moods. He remains the same. But Treasure is a creature of fancy. She may breeze in and ask him to go roller skating or play tennis in the closed road, she may wake him at dawn and order him to dress and go skating, she may refuse to roller skate at all. The boy can never know what to expect. His hopes are raised and dashed according to the vagaries and whims of Treasure's timetable. Then he retreats to his own sofa and watches television quietly.

There used to be fisticuffs when they were little and pushings off tricycles and fights over the Tarzan swing, but now Treasure and the boy are more sophisticated.

I return home one freezing evening to see the Treasure rushing about the pavement in a frenzy. 'Harry is stuck,' she tells me, fighting hysteria. 'You've got to help him.' I approach the front gate. There is the top half of the Perez boy sticking out of our coal hole. He is pale and frozen but smiling bravely. Treasure had forgotten her keys and they had remembered how they used to climb down the coal hole when young.

The boy bravely went first but got stuck half way. He forgot he had grown bigger. And now here he is, his waist in a vice, his legs dangling below helplessly. I try to pull him out. He winces with pain and grits his teeth in a chappish way.

'You've got to get him out,' says Treasure, whirling round the coal hole in a fright.

I rush down to the basement trying to think of a plan before calling the fire brigade. This is a tense moment. There are his legs dangling down. I pile boxes underneath them. Treasure and I reassure him from above and below respectively. With his feet supported he can at last push himself up and free. He is suffering from exposure and embarrassment. He runs home blushing very slightly. It is at times like this that he endears himself to Treasure.

Treasure does her homework

Treasure has strange difficulties with French. She cannot for the life of her remember a single verb. After two years of study she is still stumped by conjunctions. Only last week she forgot the French version of 'and'. She can remember the lyrics of the entire works of Madness, every word of a one-hour telephone call and several dozen Italian obscenities learnt on holiday, rather like a highly skilled parrot, but she cannot remember French. Treasure is only selectively self-motivated.

'Help me,' she screams Führer-like from the living room. 'You've got to help me.' She is crimson with panic. 'I can't do it without you. Stay here.'

I stay, testing verbs and vocabulary. Is Treasure pretending to be thick as two planks? Is this a genuine difficulty? Treasure recites her French phonetically with a heavy English accent, ever so loudly with a thunderous expression. Wrong every time. No amount of repetition improves things. How does the teacher manage? I cannot fault her. She is French, charming, has the patience of a saint and impeccable taste in earrings. Treasure will never benefit from a united Europe.

'Try writing it down four times each bit,' I say, in what I feel to be a helpful and sympathetic tone. But sharp as a tack Treasure notices that beneath the mask of civilised and supportive parent there lurks a disappointed, enraged and pushy mother.

'You think I'm stupid,' she shrieks wildly. 'Go away. Just leave me alone. Why can't you help me properly? Why not?'

I leave Treasure alone. Her screams become more desperate. 'Come back. You've got to help me.'

Dare I re-enter the room? I feel close to a heart attack – thudding pulse, bursting blood vessels, difficulty breathing. Other parents are able to help their children in a calm supportive way, but I am not. I realise that Treasure is in an unenviable position. She is an adolescent girl with a menopausal and volatile mother. Breathing deeply and trying to emulate a grown-up, I return to the torture chamber. Treasure is collapsed in a scattered nest of homework on the floor, red from weeping. She has stamped on her fifth protractor and broken it.

Treasure and I, emotionally exhausted, stop for *East-Enders* and Rescue Remedy. Treasure has a hot choc and her teddy. She is an invalid recovering from trauma. At the end of *EastEnders* she weakly recites a verb.

'I can remember it,' she whispers. She eats a banana. She is gathering strength. Bravely she staggers from the sofa to the carpet and writes out more French. By bedtime we are both ever so pleasant.

Thrown off guard by Treasure's affectionate attitude   31

over the last hour and a half, I lean over to kiss her good-night.

'Don't kiss me,' she begs, desperate, shrinking into a corner of her bed. 'Where is it? Where is it?' she whispers, scrabbling wildly at her bedside shelf. 'My inhaler. Where is it? You smell so horrible you've given me asthma.'

Treasure lies back on her pillows like a consumptive poet. 'What have you been eating?' She puffs at her inhaler and moans quietly. Is it the spring onions or is she gearing up for a day off school? Tomorrow is the French test.

Feeding Treasure

Treasure is infuriated by my store of apple juice.

'You've got three types of apple juice here.' She is Poirot discovering strychnine. The television has informed her that apple juice gives you cancer and she now realises that I am casually allowing her to be poisoned.

'You don't care,' she shrieks. 'I'll get cancer.'

'Don't be silly,' say I calmly. 'It's only the cloudy sort that might be risky. Just those two little cartons.'

'Oh that's right,' shouts Treasure in a sarcastic tone. 'Just the ones I've been drinking all week. You're so mean you'd rather I die than throw anything away.'

Treasure is sensitive to food issues. She is often a vegetarian on moral grounds. As roast gravy dinners are her absolute favourite, this means a period of abstinence and self-denial, which is not mood-enhancing. I wouldn't mind, but Treasure loathes potatoes, pulses, nuts, Mediterranean vegetables and cheese sauce. This rather limits her diet. She must live, when vegetarian, almost exclusively on pasta and grated cheese and becomes paler and more bad-tempered by the day.

33

Last time we were almost saved by Mrs Perez's buffet lunch. Treasure succumbed to a chicken drumstick, delicately marinaded in ginger, garlic and soya sauce.

'Shall I have another?' she asked. 'Does it matter?'

'No,' I said, desperate for her to swallow lumps of protein. 'Be a vegetarian tomorrow.' Treasure ate two more drumsticks and some slabs of delicious ham. But she had overdone it and was overcome with stomach ache and remorse on the way home.

'Why did you let me do that? Why? You should have stopped me.'

She was bent double at the front door. 'Let me in,' she screamed, her strange position blocking my access to the keyhole.

'You're in the way. I can't open the door.'

'I hate you. You don't care. I'll never eat meat again.'

But now we do – free-range or organic. Tonight we are having chops.

'I don't want chops,' says Treasure, looking vaguely green. In his youth her grandpa was able to go green at will and she has inherited his skills. 'I don't want anything. I'll just have salad. And water,' says she ominously.

I give up on the chops. I make myself an omelette – a lovely fluffy mushroom one just the right size for me. Treasure spots it.

'Can I have some?'

'No. It's my omelette. You didn't want anything.' I am aiming at consistency again. Treasure is appalled.

'Other parents feed their children,' says she snottily and sticks her nose in the air but the smell of my omelette gets up it. 'You're so selfish. Can't I have a bit? Just give me that corner. And you didn't say omelette. You said chops.'

Treasure is right. I misled her. Swayed by this final accusation I give up my attempt at consistency. I give her a section of my omelette.

A mistake. Saying goodnight I notice the wasted omelette in her bedroom, cold and ruined. I shout at Treasure until she eats up the hated thing. We are on the road to eating disorders.

Another day over but the chops are still lurking in the fridge. I am becoming obsessed by them. I try them again the next day but Treasure has secretly snatched one of Grandma's fish cakes for breakfast, the last of our supplies sent up from Hove. She is sickened by the mention of any more food. The chops will fester and go to waste. Stacks of unwanted food and drink are mounting up.

I begin to feel nostalgic for the vegetarian days. One is not so pressurised by a deep frozen vegeburger. It cannot rot in the fridge like a chop.

The Wonderbra

Treasure is desperate for a Gossard Wonderbra. Lizzie has one so she must have one. I am rather impressed by Treasure's confidence in her physical self. At her age I had no bosom at all and wanted a flat chest forever. When it grew I hid it in large jumpers and stooped about feeling silly. But here is Treasure boldly demanding a Wonderbra.

There are none left in Holloway. All the world wants one, so we go to Fenwicks. Tragedy. There are still none in Treasure's size. But she cannot bear to leave the shop without one.

'You get one Mum,' begs the Treasure. 'Go on. Try one on.'

I try one. I try with and without the extra bits of padding. Either way the Wonderbra looks ever so rude. It produces two balloons up by my neck. I look like something out of Playboy. Treasure is thrilled.

'Buy it Mum,' she orders. 'You must buy it.'

'It looks silly,' I say, secretly rather impressed with my new look. I obviously need a selection of smart new brassieres. Treasure summons the assistant.

'Madam does not need a Wonderbra,' says the assistant strictly. 'Madam has a natural cleavage.' Treasure is thrilled to bits. So am I. I try on more glamorous brassieres. The lady assistant returns.

'Madam is so slender,' says she in an admiring way. This is not a word that has ever been applied to me in the past. The praise rather goes to my head. I purchase two Passionata brassieres, one black, one white, and matching knickers with lacy bits.

Treasure is rather pleased with herself. On her instigation I have been transformed from frump to glamourpuss. She has memorised the entire brassiere department script, which she recites en route to the car.

'Madam is so slender,' says Treasure repeatedly. She doesn't even care about her own lack of Wonderbra. She is selfless. We will order her one. This is one of our more successful outings.

Treasure visits her grandparents

Treasure leads a life of drudgery illuminated only by the weekends.

'Don't ask me about school. Stop it,' she shouts dramatically, poking her fingers into her ears. 'My life is at the weekends.'

This is a bad patch for Treasure. She rises daily from her bed snarling, refuses breakfast and neglects her homework and goldfish. She is wrecking her health. She will not eat or sleep enough. She thinks, breathes and dreams Weekend. Hysterical with exhaustion she twirls from day to day, pausing only for a brief slump in front of Antipodean soaps, strong enough only to phone and plan weekends and irritate the dog.

I decide to force Treasure to rest – to whisk her to Hove to visit Grandma and Grandpa. Treasure, in her pleasanter moods, is the light of their lives. They have stocked up with her favourite dinners, cakes and exotic fruits in an optimistic way, to delight their grandchild.

Treasure is decimated by my plan. 'I'm not going,' she shouts crossly. 'I won't be able to see my friends. And what about my job? I can't go. I can't.' She clings to the telephone for consolation.

We compromise. Treasure can stay all night at Rosie's on Friday and slave at the mini-market until two on Saturday, and then I'll scoop her up in the car and drive her to the seaside.

I collect her at the appointed time. She is unable to speak in the car. She has only the energy to change radio channels and cassette tracks every few seconds. Sometimes only one second of tune will send her finger shooting to the button. Click – snatch of tune – click – a chord – click. Amid the swirling traffic of the Elephant and Castle Treasure settles for manic techno-rock. It seems to relax her.

Soon it lulls her to sleep. I turn the hideous cacophony down but she wakes up at once, demanding that her lullaby be turned up again. She snoozes on.

Arriving in Hove she still has little strength. She knows she is missing an evening's bopping at the Strobe. Wearily she sinks into Grandma's armchair in front of the telly, dressed in black rags and requesting silence – a tragic figure. Grandma is desolate. She longs for the chubby, smiling, pudgy-faced Treasure of the past. Grandpa is off to the betting shop.

Leaving the family settled in this way I take the dog for a walk, meet a chum and end up in the pub. This is not a wise move. I ring to ask when dinner will be ready.

'It's ready now,' barks Grandma. 'Where are you? She's been nagging for an hour, "Where's Mummy?"' Grandma is emotionally torn. She is keen for me to have a social life but not thrilled with her role of childminder to a grump. Treasure is also emotionally torn. She loves her grandma but she also loves the Strobe. It sparkles in her memory. She now imagines only its delights, not the crowds, drugs, stifling heat and possible death by trampling that rather marred her last visit.

Her bate has intensified during the evening, naturally, because while she's been sitting alone sixty miles from happiness, I've been out playing with my friends. She becomes dissatisfied with the choice of telly programme. Expressing her opinion in the usual venomous way, Treasure stamps from the room.

Grandma is horrified. She grabs for her angina spray, unaccustomed to the vocabulary of modern youth. But Treasure has fallen asleep again. She sleeps and slumps her way through the weekend, waking now and again to spray herself with Grandma's perfume or paint her nails in blue and red checks.

On the way home Treasure shows signs of life. The stench of Holloway revives her completely. Messages twinkle from the answerphone. Recharged, she embarks upon an orgy of telephoning, planning, visiting and screeching. Fortified by the Rest Cure she is back on course. *Her* course.

Treasure on holiday

It is boys and shopping that help Treasure and I to endure our holiday together. She is sick at Gatwick, sick at Malpensa and flops inertly about Milan stultified by the heat and humidity and weakened by sickness. For a day or so Treasure can only lay about our friend's flat reading Adrian Mole and startled by the ceaseless explicit sanitary towel adverts and rude pop videos on Italian TV. She is thrilled by the lack of censorship.

There is nothing much else of interest for her here anyway. She isn't keen on the fascist architecture or the Plague Victims' Enclosure, only the cool air-conditioned shops in the town centre. She whizzes into Fiorucci and pokes about for hours. I am bored to death.

But Venice perks her up tremendously. It is full of shops crammed with sparkly little glass souvenirs. Treasure tolerates the water bus, ignores St Marks and rushes for the shops and stalls, darting in and out, maddened by excess. She embarks on an orgy of buying.

She is desperate for a glass spider with very thin legs that will break at once in the suitcase. She settles for a

41

family of glass mice, vulgar sweets for friends, gondolier earrings, apple strudel and, triumph of the day, a Chevignon T-shirt at knock-down price. Then she wants a baseball hat, the sort easily found in the Holloway Road and sported by yobbos. I balk at the baseball hat. It is cheap and nasty and nothing to do with Venice.

'Tony Lupman wears those,' I snap, naming the boy she most hates.

'But I really need one.' Treasure looks hot and desperate. 'It's my pocket money. Why can't I buy one?'

I cannot allow it. Here we are, surrounded by magnificence and art and buying a hideous baseball hat. My legs ache from loitering in a thousand gift shops.

'I want, I want, I want,' I shout at Treasure, drawing attention to our little squabble. Passing tourists are entranced.

'I hate you,' she hisses. 'You're so embarrassing. Why are you so horrible to me?'

Humidity is ninety eight, temperature somewhere up in the thousands, the sun beating down. I realise, midshriek, that the baseball hat is probably Treasure's most sensible request.

'Alright. Buy the bloody baseball hat. Do what you like.' But it is too late.

'I don't want it now.' Treasure stamps off in her giant black trainers.

We press on with our holiday, to Sardinia. Treasure and I and Italian teenager Valeria are to go on a boat trip round the coast. *My* friend can't come, she has a stomach ache. Valeria cannot swim, she has a period. In Italy it is considered unwise to swim with a period. If Valeria won't swim, Treasure won't swim. Both sit in the shade of the lower deck pecking in turn at Treasure's Gameboy. They do not speak. They ignore the azure limpid sea and silver beaches.

'Mummy, can't you go somewhere else?' Treasure is intensely embarrassed by my new leopard-skin patterned bikini.

I move away. I read my book and sit in the sun in the hated bikini, I talk to Italian mummies, I swim obediently at the chosen beaches, plunge from the boat into turquoise lagoons. At the third beach I call to Treasure. 'Are you coming swimming?'

'No Mummy,' she says crossly, sitting with Valeria in the gloom. She looks pained. 'Please leave me alone. I know what I want.' She glances with pity at my bikini. 'Just go away Mummy.' She is whispering through closed lips rather like a ventriloquist, keen that no one realises we are related.

I go away. I remain calm. Treasure is, after all, burnt lobster-red in patches from yesterday, our first day sunbathing, when she refused to cover herself in sunblock, T-shirt and long skirt. Perhaps it's a good job she is staying in the shade. Perhaps the drillion-lire boat trip is not a total waste of effort and money.

I am allowed to sit next to Treasure and Valeria at lunchtime but am encouraged, by withering looks, not to speak. Seafood pasta is provided free, water a thousand lire a glass.

On to the next beach. Off I go into the limpid waters. Swimming among the thousand tourists also delivered by boat, I suddenly encounter Treasure in the water. 'Hallo Mummy.' She is smiling pleasantly and has found another friend, Gabriela, to go swimming with.

43

I sunbathe alone. Treasure passes with her girl-friends. 'We're going back to the boat,' says she cheerily. Lying down, my bikini perhaps seems less offensive. Treasure's mood has magically lightened. She even returns later in a concerned way to make sure I don't miss the boat.

Back on it once more Treasure and her friends go up on to the sunny top deck. Baffled by her pleasant behaviour I climb up the ladder to spy briefly. Treasure and her friends are surrounded by boys. This trip seems to be a success. New friends have been made, photos taken, addresses exchanged. The boys disembark on the mainland, blowing kisses. But Treasure is planning a sequel.

'Can we go and see those boys Mummy? You can drive us. It's only this far on the map.' She indicates an eighty-mile trip. I refuse. Treasure is outraged.

'But they asked us. Why not? You can leave us there and pick us up later.'

'No.'

'Why are you so horrid to me?' rages Treasure, baffled. 'You spoil everything.'

Treasure is not too excited about beautiful deserted beaches or our holiday, until she discovers that at night she and Valeria may go to the piazza alone. The piazza is full of boys; handsome Italian ones and young American males, stuck out here for years in the navy, lonely, homesick and hated by the Sards. They are thrilled by the arrival of Treasure and Valeria and over the moon that Treasure speaks English. They are unaware that she is thirteen and a half and buy her Martinis.

Treasure's holiday perks up no end. The piazza is full of boys *and* shops. She is in heaven. She is unaware that my friend and I often keep watch from a concealed café table. Treasure endures her day on the baking silver beaches, grills herself dangerously in the sun, swims in the limpid waters and waits for evening in the piazza.

Soon she and Valeria learn that there exists, somewhere miles along the deserted coast road, a thrilling disco. Can she and Valeria go? Please, please. Can they go on motorbikes with Italian youths at midnight and come back at 5 a.m.?

I am frozen with terror. I know that Sardinia is littered not only with rapists, but also kidnappers. Only weeks ago the troops were moved in to rescue a child mistaken for a relative of the Aga Khan and snatched by bandits. Mr Khan lives just a few miles away. They may mistake Treasure, she may fall off a motorbike. I am keen to handcuff Treasure to my wrist for the remainder of the holiday.

My friend is more sensible. She is not Treasure's mother and has worked as a youth leader and maintained perfect discipline. She takes charge. 'I shall ask Valeria's mother tonight on the phone,' says she reasonable as anything, 'but I know she'll say no to motorbikes.'

Valeria's mother does say no to motorbikes. She says yes to us driving them there at midnight, waiting for three hours and bringing them home at three. 'It's only fair,' says my friend. 'They must have one disco.'

We take them. Treasure and Valeria bounce off into the disco and disappear into the milling crowds. Music throbs, lights flicker and flask. For my friend it is instant migraine. We retire to a quiet bar. The disco is situated in   45 a smart new marina, so we have our best frocks on. I am wearing a black worm dress lent by my friend. I feel rather chic. She is wearing a silvery number. We receive rather odd looks. We are perhaps mistaken for ladies of the night. The bar closes. We move to the lobby of a classy hotel. It closes. We return to the hellish discotheque. There are Treasure and Valeria bopping away, surrounded by youths. We wander on around the deserted marina. It is chilly, we have forgotten our cardigans, it is still only two o'clock.

In the darkness we detect a pile of deckchairs on a jetty looking out to sea. Too late my friend screams a warning, 'Mind the rock.'

I fall over it – a particularly vicious rock which stabs me in the leg. I shriek horrible obscenities across the beautiful moonlit seascape. I am in excruciating pain. For some reason this amuses my friend.

'One minute you're standing up,' she weeps with laughter, 'next minute you're on the floor.' She feels that the sophisticated dress rather enhances the joke. We sit gazing out to sea until 3 a.m., two elderly chaperones, one with a bleeding leg, waiting to collect Treasure and Valeria.

Treasure is ecstatic when collected, and wet through.

'This boy threw me in the pool four times,' says she. 'He wouldn't even let me take my shoes off.' She has had the time of her life. It was worth it – the hours of wandering, the bleak bars, the hostile looks, the wounded leg. Treasure is loving her holiday.

Summer

The weather is now very hot. Hosepipes are banned and the gardens are beginning to shrivel. On the Heath the gardeners are perversely shaving the grass so short that it turns yellow in patches. But they go on cutting it and cutting it, even the bits that have been left long and wild in previous years. Nobody can understand why. I meet another dog owner stamping across the stubble and we revile the gardeners together. I ask a keeper the reason and he tells me it makes it easier to pick up the rubbish.

This plan doesn't seem to be working. The remains of picnics lie in piles and bits all over the bald lawns blighting the area, and the dogs are seduced and delayed by leftovers, leaving their own excrement dotted here and there. I pick up my own dog's poo in plastic bags. Picking it up one day beside the tennis courts, I notice that all players have stopped to cheer. They regard me as a paragon among dog owners.

Only the Ladies' Pond remains green and restful. Once inside it one feels less crabby and sweaty. No men or boys are allowed, not even babies. No noise, no transistors, no rowdiness. The pool is enclosed, protected from the squalor of the rest of London. Nothing disturbs its tranquillity, not even the odd Peeping Tom crouching behind the slatted fences and bushes, squinting at bosoms on the distant lawns.

At home we try lunch in the garden, but wasps swirl around the table and fall into the drinks making Treasure squeal and run indoors, into the cool living room and soothing flicker of the television. On hot summer days she likes to be indoors with the curtains drawn. She prefers winter for running about outdoors in a scoop-neck T-shirt.

At Treasure's school towards the end of summer term, Salbutamol inhalers are all the rage, perhaps because of the pollen count. Lola Dickinson uses hers all the time, says Treasure. At the slightest wheeze out it comes, puff puff down her throat. She offers it round. She offered it to Treasure but Treasure refused, honestly she did. She knew she mustn't use someone else's inhaler. Treasure promises she's never taken any. But she knows she *must* have one of her own. She has diagnosed herself.

'But I do get asthma. I do. I need an inhaler.' Lola has one, Charlotte has one, Karen has two. Everybody has one.

Treasure's inherited temperament

Treasure is a determined creature. I wonder if she has inherited this trait from Grandma. Grandma will battle fiercely for her rights, even against terrifying opponents. Grandpa caught her battling with a female punk on the seafront promenade the other day. She had been sitting on a bench in the sun looking out to sea next to this pair of punks when the male hurls his beer can over the wall on to the beach. A cry goes up from the sunbathers beneath. Up jumps a lady in her swimming costume. 'Who threw that?'

'Nothing to do with me,' lied the punk.

Grandma felt impelled to speak. 'Well nobody else did it,' she roared.

'Shut up you silly old bag,' replied the female. Grandma was naturally incensed.

'Don't you speak to me like that,' she snapped, raising her walking stick.

'I'll push that stick down your bloody throat,' shouted the female punk rather aggressively and grabbed the stick. Grandma hung on boldly and just at that point, with the two ladies grappling and pulling at the stick, Grandpa reappeared from his stroll and bravely separated them. He escorted Grandma home.

'She shouldn't get so excited,' he says to me rather glumly later. 'It's dangerous.'

Grandma's food supplies

One of Grandma's major concerns is our diet. She likes to supplement it whenever she can with superior produce from Hove. On each of our visits she packs a large container of foodstuffs: fruit pies, fish cakes, smoked salmon pieces, soups and fresh fish from the seaside. Grandma's cooking is of a tremendously high standard. Her fish and chips, cakes and pastries and roast dinners are paradise. For a few days after our visit to Hove, the fridge is heaven. We eat up all our presents.

Grandpa, however, is often ungrateful and disobedient. He is not always lavish with his praise, sometimes only grunting the odd syllable at table or losing his appetite at crucial feeding times. Contrary to the doctor's strict instructions (following numerous heart attacks), he *will* eat salt. Grandma cannot control him. If denied salty foods he will stagger to the shops for stinking kippers, bacon and sausages and cook them himself late at night. He will spray his food with extra salt, he will drink whisky and he will not eat his greens.

Grandma screams with temper. It does her no good. 51

He has taken out his hearing aid and put on his walk-man.

Sometimes, to relieve the tension, Grandpa comes to town for a couple of days.

'I can't stand it,' says he in a heart-rending way. 'Your mother is driving me mad. I cannot live with her three hundred and fifty four days in a year. I've got to get away.' He comes to our house. He attends the local betting shop. He washes up scrupulously. He is happy for a few hours, but then the noise, the mess, the Treasure and I begin to get on his nerves.

'You and your daughter are driving me mad,' says he. 'I've had enough.' For a moment he looks beaten, but then he remembers his responsibilities. 'And I can't leave your mother alone.'

Before leaving he has bacon, sausage, egg, beans and toast for breakfast. Then a hot choc and doughnut at Victoria Station. He has twirled his beard forward and goes off back to Hove looking rather smart.

Treasure and the neighbours

Treasure is to go on a sponsored Dogathon for a deserving animal charity. She and Lizzie rush up and down the street asking the neighbours to sponsor them. Both whirl back half an hour later in a state of shock. Anthea Big-Bottom on the corner has refused to co-operate. Treasure and Lizzie are outraged.

'Anthea Big-Bottom is disgusting,' shouts Treasure. 'I hate her. How can she be so mean?' Anthea has dared to say that she doesn't believe in such things.

I must admit that I too am shocked by Anthea's behaviour. She, until now, has been animal saviour of the street. She has adopted sick and scabrous pets, loved them wildly and revived them. She has sneaked to the RSPCA about suspiciously skinny cats and chained-up dogs and summoned the police at once when Mr Harris next door kicked some occupied rabbit cages about the garden. Now here she is refusing to contribute to the Dogathon. Treasure is determined in future to sneer openly at her in the street. She will not observe social conventions and say hallo, or respect Anthea's right to an opinion.

53

There was a time when Treasure was polite to neighbours, even Anthea. We had been invited into Anthea's garden to see how our poxy rabbit was progressing. She had been dabbing ointment lovingly on its sores for weeks and now it was fat and furry again and we had come to admire it. Treasure, seven years old, smiled sweetly and her little plaits stuck out. But just two feet to the right of her head hung Anthea's gargantuan knickers.

Would the Treasure make an offensive remark? Would she laugh rudely? No. Not the tiniest smirk or funny look. Only out in the street again did Treasure feel free to comment. 'What big knickers,' she said, her eyes wide and blue. 'Hasn't Anthea got a big bottom?' She had demonstrated immense self-control and perfect manners. I was ever so proud. What a charming age. Too young for value judgements, old enough for sensitivity. Treasure wouldn't stoop to being such a creep nowadays. Worn down by years of noise nuisance and Treasure's audacity, the weaker neighbours greet us with a frozen smile. The stronger ones complain.

This evening Treasure enrages Mrs Perez. There is Mrs P after a hard day's work, plodding quietly up to the living room with her tray of supper, when the phone rings. It is Treasure at the home of a friend and infuriated that she cannot get through to me on the phone. In her absence I have grabbed the opportunity to use it myself. Treasure orders Mrs Perez to run round with a message, quite forgetting to say please.

'Doesn't she make your blood boil?' asks Mrs P later. I am surprised at her question. She has seen me simmering away over the years, boiling over, disturbing the street. But now she has just tried to reprimand

Treasure herself and ended up trembling with fury. She expected a tiny bit of contrition, perhaps even an apology. She forgot that Treasure has her own unique view of events in which she, the innocent victim, is always wrongly accused by deranged elderly inquisitors.

Some of these monsters have sponsored the Dogathon. It was easy to collect sponsors. Faced suddenly by two smiling, polite and altruistic girls, the neighbours thoughtlessly signed away their money. Now, days later, their mornings disturbed by shrieking, their nights by Treasure and her chums carousing home from the Strobe in the early hours, they may not be too keen to cough up. But Treasure has lost interest in the Dogathon for some reason. She does not wish to collect her spoils. She hasn't time at the moment. She and Daisy are busy planning the 24-Hour Sponsored Fast.

Treasure and the critics

I leave Treasure alone with the grandparents for fifteen minutes while I walk the dog. When I return they are all squabbling fiercely. There has been a contretemps over television programmes.

Grandma had rushed into the living room and snapped off Treasure's gripping documentary in favour of *Mastermind*, Grandpa's favourite programme. But as he was snoozing on the sofa and is partially deaf, Grandma blasted rather than switched it on, bellowing 'It's *Mastermind*', in a voice of thunder. Grandpa awoke to an inferno – *Mastermind* booming, Grandma roaring and Treasure shrieking with shock and disappointment. This is the situation I find upon my return.

It is Treasure's second shriek of the day. She had another one during my afternoon dog walk because she awoke from her nap with a raging thirst and Grandpa opened the packet of orange juice too slowly. No wonder he is peeved. Later, when Treasure and Grandma are slightly more subdued, Grandpa criticises.

'Of course I don't blame *her*,' he tells me, with a

resigned and damning look. 'It's you. You've spoilt her.' He returns to his armchair with a comforting book on World War Two.

This is a popular criticism which I often encounter.

'She's spoilt,' says another visitor to our home, lips clamped. Treasure had called loudly from upstairs.

'MUM.'

I have told her never to do this. She must come downstairs and speak rather than stay upstairs and roar. I have sworn that I will not answer distant roaring. She roars on.

'MUM.' I do not answer. I try to continue my chat with the visitor. The roaring continues. Visitor's views are reinforced. And now Treasure cannot enter the kitchen and speak normally even if she wants to. She has embarrassed herself. She hides on the staircase and calls again in a commanding way.

'MUM. I can't find my homework diary. Will you just help me look for it.'

Visitor is gripped by this drama. Will I feebly help Treasure or will I sensibly refuse and instruct her to search again? But this time I am in luck. I know where the diary is. I can inform her in a moderate voice and avert disaster.

'It's on top of the piano.'

Treasure disappears. No more roaring. Visitor is deprived of a treat, but it makes no difference. He is already convinced that the damage is done. All critics know that had *they* been Mummy, things would have been different.

Theirs is a final judgement. Spoilt means done for, with no hope of a cure, and Treasure plays into their hands. She can detect a critic from two floors up as if by radar. At the first whiff of disapproval she will switch like lightning to rebellious mode, sulking, sneering and flouncing about, confirming the critic's views. She will pull out all the stops: horrid table manners, offensive language, dull answers. Any glimmer of altruism, charm, wit and a better nature will be stifled and the critic will be thrilled. They were right after all. I have made a hash of being Mummy.

Grown-ups behaving badly

I feel that I, like Treasure, have inherited Grandma's temperament. I find it difficult to contain myself in public when confronted by what I consider to be an injustice. I came across one only the other day in the bank. There was a queue of eighteen people and only one functioning cashier. A quick stare around the premises revealed fourteen bank staff diddling about doing other things.

I asked loudly whether there was any possibility that one or two of the milling crowd of bank employees might come and attend to the customers. The rest of the queue looked rather embarrassed. Only one man spoke up in agreement.

'You wouldn't get this in Germany,' he roared. 'The Germans get things done.' I was disappointed in my only ally.

Luckily Treasure was not with me. She hates a squabble in public. She is keen for me to be polite even in the face of intense provocation. I may not, on any account, be critical or abusive even when faced with

59

the cockiest and most offensive shopkeeper or public employee or mile-long queue. Nor may I be high-spirited or uninhibited when out and about.

Treasure came to the cinema with Mrs H and me this week to see an acclaimed and rather adult film. She was shocked to find that Mrs H also behaved rather badly in public. Her own mother is not the only one. Mrs H was loudly reviling her neighbour.

'She's always going to parties,' shouted Mrs H, stamping about the cinema foyer pulling dreadful faces. 'She's obsessed with parties. And clubs. Her and her bloody clubs.'

Mrs H and I laughed loudly and unconstrainedly and bought a giant popcorn to share. Treasure kept her distance, glancing at us now and then in a slightly disgusted way and bought her own small popcorn separately, disassociating herself as much as possible.

Mrs H and I were then electrified by the adverts, Mrs H being particularly keen on a saucy jeans advert and on the milk flake and deodorant ones that followed. We laughed like anything and commented and grovelled in the popcorn carton. It all reminded Mrs H of her youth when she used to be fascinated by popular culture.

Treasure behaved the best. She sat quietly and ate her popcorn politely without spilling any. We all found the film rather gripping. Mrs H nudged me and glanced rather nervously at Treasure in the more terrifying and adult scenes, but Treasure never batted an eyelid. This was probably *Blue Peter* compared to some of the nightmare videos that Treasure and her chums have watched during low key evenings at home. It was the staggering denouement that had most worried Mrs H. Once out in the foyer again she and I blabbed about it in an animated way as we passed the queue, inadvertently wrecking things for the next audience.

Treasure was appalled. She raised her eyes to heaven. 'You two are mad,' said she, while walking rather elegantly towards the car.

Treasure the lifesaver

There is an unpleasant smell coming from Treasure's room. It can be detected even through the stench of jos-sticks that she has taken to burning. Hidden somewhere among the mountains of clothes and bits something must have died, or an ancient snack must lie concealed and forgotten.

'Can you smell something funny in here?' I ask as pleasantly as possible.

'No I can't,' snaps Treasure. 'What is your problem?' She lights more jossticks in a fury. She has taken my enquiry as a personal affront. But later a scream of distress rends the news headlines. Treasure is calling for help. I rush upstairs. The cause of the mysterious odour is revealed. There, lying on its side, wiggling feebly and gasping its last, the largest goldfish is fighting for its life in foetid water.

Leaning over the tank to examine the tragedy the ghastly stink hit me in the nose. It is perhaps a decade since Treasure has cleaned out the fish's home. Through the murk two more goldfish, made of sterner stuff, are still upright. An emergency rescue is staged, the two swimmers transferred to a pan, the near fatality to the washbasin.

Treasure is heartbroken and racked with guilt. 'I didn't neglect them, did I? I did look after them.'

'Well not really.' Even Treasure realises that I cannot lie. She has never been able to clean out pets. She is desperate to have them but forgets that each one is a tiny excrement factory. The guinea-pigs had a rough time as well. Not only did they produce truckloads of malodorous waste matter but also reproduced themselves in a flash and contracted a noxious skin disease. All eleven had to be shampooed and blowdried daily and have ointment rubbed on to the nasty patches. This became my summer holiday task.

Now we have the mouldering goldfish. But Treasure is older and more capable. She slaves away, washing the tank, borrowing and boiling new gravel, attending to the casualty in the basin. I pour some Rescue Remedy in next to its nose. It rights itself for a second.

'It's getting better,' squeaks Treasure. She scrubs fiercely at the tank and cleans the reeking, slimy ornaments. The fish lies sideways, barely able to flap. Treasure goes to bed repentant, her love of goldfish renewed. For months now they have been overshadowed by boys and the Strobe. Only this rather dramatic statement by the largest one has reminded Treasure of their existence and requirements.

I awake expecting to find a corpse in the basin, but no. The goldfish has recovered. It is swimming perkily upright. I have saved its life. I feel a glow of achievement. A vet's life must be tremendously rewarding.

I wake Treasure up with the happy news *and* a teen magazine.

'Leave me alone,' she snarls in her usual morning mode. I had foolishly expected a brighter response – as Treasure jumped from her bed and rushed eagerly to see her fish, saved from the jaws of death. Eventually she staggers to the bathroom.

'I saved it,' she croaks.

'What do you mean, *you* saved it?'

'Well didn't you hear me last night? I went down later, about eleven o'clock, and put a junior soluble aspirin in. It made bubbles. That's what saved it.'

Treasure is enormously proud. She has grabbed the glory for herself. *She* wants the glow of achievement.

Saving the dinner

The doorbell rings. It is Mr Perez. 'I'm locked out,' says he. 'Please may I come in and wait here?' Not feeling too well he had staggered out to buy cigarettes and inadvertently forgotten his keys. The trouble is that Mrs Perez is at church and has left a delicious bean casserole in the oven which Mr Perez was to turn off in fifteen minutes. She was up till 1 a.m. preparing and grilling bits of aubergine and pepper and now there she is, up at the church, and when she gets home her lovely lunch will be burnt to a crisp.

I leave Mr Perez chain smoking in the kitchen and drive to the church. Treasure is not pleased. The smoke offends her and she cannot get at her breakfast while Mr Perez sits in his cloud of smoke in the kitchen. But this is an emergency. Mrs Perez's creation must be saved.

I arrive at the church and enter, mid-service. I have forgotten to change out of my dog-walking outfit. I creep towards the back pew, a mud-covered infidel. This is a novelty for me. It is a novelty for the congregation. They all have a stare. Kindly one of them offers me a

65

hymnbook. I explain my quest, mentioning a sick husband locked out of his home. I cannot see Mrs Perez anywhere. Together the hymnbook man and I creep along the aisles searching. People are staring like anything.

At last I spot her, right over the other side at the front. The man summons her while I hide behind a pillar. The sermon continues.

Mrs Perez appears in a terrible flap, suspecting a fatal accident. She heard 'knocked out' instead of 'locked out'. I tell her about the trapped casserole. She is in her car and off down the road in a flash to save it, and to remove Mr P from our kitchen. He is in for a wigging when she returns. Again and again the husbands on our side fail to measure up to the husbands over the road.

Treasure's attitude to clothing

I have dressed rather smartly, I feel, to go to Treasure's
parents' evening – chic black number, very respectable
length, best shoes, muted make-up, matching accessories.

Although glued to the phone, Treasure spots me on
the way out. 'Oh God!' she shrieks. 'My mother.' She
places her hand over the mouthpiece. 'You're not going
like that? You can't be.' She addresses the telephone
again. 'My God. My mother looks like a prostitute.'

This description is totally inaccurate. Treasure is
rarely satisfied with my appearance. Casual wear comes
under the blanket description of bag lady, smart outfits
are classified as prostitute.

She takes particular exception to ensembles involv-
ing leggings.

'Please, not the three layers. Please,' she begs. 'You're
not wearing your socks like that?' She rolls her eyes. 'You
can't. Turn them down.' She has rigid views on turn-ups
and downs. 'Turn your jeans down,' she snaps. 'People
will say, "Who's that silly lady making her jeans look too
short?" I'm not coming with you like that.'

'Walk ten paces ahead,' I say. 'Pretend I'm not your mother.' We have had many such walks, the grimmest near to school.

But although disgusted by my attire, Treasure is keen to borrow bits of it, especially black bits, jeans or smartest knickers. And once the clothes are off the body, Treasure's attitude towards them becomes somewhat cavalier, almost reckless. The clothes are quickly lost, lent and generally scattered about. She has a new penchant for swapping clothes with friends. In our house we have some visiting T-shirts, spotty socks and green jeans. My black T-shirt is off in Stoke Newington, Treasure's new jumper is locked in the Strobe cloakroom, her Doc Martens are in Crouch End and her school shoes are nowhere on earth. She often limps about in ill-fitting borrowed shoes and sports large blisters.

She has been desperate to get rid of the hated school shoes for months and now she's cleverly lost them. Rosie swears she left them in the hall, Treasure swears she couldn't find them. I am suddenly infuriated by all the scattered clothing and this Great Shoe Mystery. I drive at top speed to Rosie's house and order a search. Rosie and Treasure search sullenly. I am the vilest mother of the year. No shoes, but a hint that they may be at Chloe's. Mansell-like, I drive to Chloe's.

'Please don't shout,' begs Treasure. 'Don't be rude to Chloe's mother.'

'I'm not going to shout,' I scream. Smiling pleasantly and with a pallid and quaking Treasure behind me, I enter Chloe's house. Yes, the shoes have been found, but they are now going round central London in the back of a car, with my black T-shirt. Chloe's calm and well-organised mummy has washed the T-shirt and the shoes will be delivered this evening. Bliss.

'Anyway,' says Treasure on the way home, 'you gave me that T-shirt.' We chatter all the way back. 'You didn't look after it / Give me my black jumper back then / It's not your jumper, it's mine / No it isn't / You've got your own one / That one's horrid . . .'

Off we go to the school play. The shoes have arrived in time. I can't see that my outfit is offensive in any way. Most of it is concealed by a tasteful grey raincoat and Liberty's wool scarf.

'Please don't wear that scarf.' Treasure is terrified. She doesn't care about its upmarket origins. She has spotted moth-holes in the left-hand corner. 'Just don't come into school with it on. Please. Just carry it.' Red with shame she rushes ahead to her place in the orchestra. From a distance I think I see her lips moving. 'Oh God. My mother.'

The goldfish
murderer

Treasure's friends have come to visit. Rosie, Andrew, Robert and a new boy. Treasure and Rosie are catering, I am up in my bedroom, an elderly recluse with the dog and the television. I appear briefly in emergencies – to find the ketchup and such like.

Treasure and Rosie come knocking at my door, pale and serious.

'Mum, can you please tell those boys to go home. They're being rude,' says Treasure mysteriously.

'What are they doing?'

I am dead keen to know what 'rude' means, but Treasure and Rosie won't tell. Omerta rules.

I ask the three boys to leave. 'Sorry boys, time to go home,' I lie brightly and pointlessly. 'I need the living room.' The boys look shocked and rather hurt. They all troop miserably into the kitchen. I return to my bedroom but soon Treasure and Rosie appear again.

'Mum,' says Treasure. 'Can those boys stay? They're being very nice now.'

'No they can't.'

'You said they could stay in the spare room. They've told their mothers.'

'They can untell their mothers.' I am aiming at consistency yet again. I am advised that consistency is an absolute must and that Treasure needs me to set boundaries. Sometimes Treasure herself signals that a boundary is required. 'Please can so-and-so stay,' she asks, with so-and-so behind her. 'Please, please!' She pulls desperate faces. These faces sometimes mean 'Say no'. After a few mistakes I can now recognise them. This time I can't tell but decide no anyway.

Treasure doesn't seem too distraught. My boundaries have worked a treat. Treasure perhaps recognises the need for a senior prefect lurking upstairs ready to jump out and control rude boys.

However the next day more boys come visiting. Robert brings another new one. He looks like a normal boy. Everyone eats a proper dinner at table under my supervision. I feel it is safe to go out for a quick drink. But there is a sudden alert. The new boy has tipped all the goldfish food into the tank.

'You've got to help us,' says Treasure, slightly frenzied. Remembering her goldfish's recent battle with death caused by rotting excess food and general filth, Treasure knows she must act at once.

'Your friends can help you,' say I ruthlessly. 'Make them clean the tank.'

Treasure puts the goldfish in the bath. Before I leave I see them swimming about in oceans of clean water. I return to find corpses. Having poured bathsalts and shampoo on to the goldfish, the murderous new boy has left.

'You've got to help us bury them,' says Treasure tragically.

I am incensed. I leave three happy fish and return to a scene of mass murder. Scooping up the dead bodies and snatching a shovel I begin to dig a burial hole in the garden.

'Why are you being so horrid to me?' Treasure is baffled. 'Why are you being so nasty?'

'I'm not very happy,' I shout, digging wildly in the dark where I hope there are no bulbs. 'Who is that boy? What sort of child is he? I want to speak to his parents. What's his phone number?'

Treasure and Rosie will not grass. Were Pol Pot a member of their peer group they would not betray him.

Treasure's best friend

Treasure's relationships are mainly tempestuous. She knows little of moderation, so a new friend is an instant best friend. It comes not just to tea after school but for Friday evening, 'and then she can stay the night and then we're going back to her house and I'll stay the night there and then we'll come back here.'

This week's best friend is Tara. 'Tara's coming to my party and can she stay the night?'

'Does her mother mind?'

'Her mother doesn't care. Her mother hates her.'

Tara is to arrive alone in the dark at the tube station. Treasure goes to meet her with the dog for protection, Tara arrives, thirteen going on twenty-three, very red lipstick, black chiffon blouse, bum-length skirt, black nylons, thigh-length Robin Hood boots. A sharp intake of breath from my adult friends helping with the party preparations. 'What mother lets a child out alone at night dressed like that?' Treasure's information must be accurate. Her mother hates her.

Next door the party begins. It rages on. Our altruistic

73

youthful neighbour has allowed Treasure the use of her flat for this disco party because I, her horrid mother, refused to have one in the house. A guest list of forty has been prepared. Treasure, after weeks of monstrous behaviour and tension, collapsed weeping on the eve of her party, terrorised by the prospect of gatecrashers. She had lost control of the guest list and no longer knew who was coming, having wildly asked millions to reassure her of her popularity and to ensure lots of presents and because it's difficult to say no.

I took over the list, cut it down, put large male bouncers on the door, bought a trolley load of pizzas, fizzy pop and snacks and we were away. But even treasure thinks Tara looks a little adult. She comes home mid-party with a hurried report.

'Tara's got a whole bottle of vodka and her own cigarettes *and* she's telling everyone she's given somebody a blow-job.' Treasure speaks of a blow-job as if it were a sandwich. I am horrified. News of such activities only reached me in my late twenties.

'Do you know what that means?'

'Course I do,' says Treasure breezily. 'I know everything.'

'Well it isn't the sort of thing even a grown-up boasts about at parties. It's private.' I feel that's a reasonably liberal comment. I'm not condemning the activity itself.

Surprisingly Treasure seems to agree. She has noticed the general disapproval. 'Nobody likes Tara,' she hisses. 'Give me the pizzas. We need more pizzas.' She twirls off, back to the party, in past the deserted living room where the DJ plays alone, through the kitchen and out into the garden where the guests have massed and are sitting on walls and standing about in the dark in slight drizzle. Why? Why aren't they bopping in the front room to the £100 disco equipment?

'Make them come in,' shouts my neighbour, exasperated. 'It's a complete waste of your money. Get them inside.'

I order them in, lock the door, hide the key, but they can't stand it. They cram themselves into the hall. We keep them penned in for several minutes but they want to go out. So the door is unlocked and they swarm back outside, probably to cluster around Tara's cigarettes, drink and tales of erotic horrors. I begin to sweep up the popcorn and spy out of the kitchen window, but Treasure spots me.

'Go away Mummy. Can't you go home?' She glares at me fiercely, white with fury, but my neighbour has had enough. She needs help. I sweep on until the end, pay the DJ (who was overweight, smelled strongly of aftershave and wasn't hip enough), smile weakly at the collecting parents and swear that it's the last party until after A levels.

Tara leaves in the morning in jeans and a jumper, looking normal, her vamp outfit in her bag, but she has left her mark behind. I find Treasure and Rosie playing The Sex Maniacs' Card Game.

'Whoever gave you that?' I snap, my voice a *mélange* of Joyce Grenfell and Hitler.

'Tara.'

I confiscate the game at once, but Treasure hardly complains.

'Can Rosie stay the night?' she asks. 'She's my best friend.'

Treasure tidies up

Treasure has begun to do tiny bits of housework voluntarily. This is unprecedented. She has tidied her room
twice in the last two weeks, I cannot imagine why. This
morning she's tidying again but she is at breaking point.
There are limits to how much of this labour she can
tolerate. Shocked and exhausted by her own efforts, she
suddenly roars for assistance.

She times her roar to coincide with my breakfast, just
as I raise the first bite of toast to my lips. I have risen at
dawn, walked the dog over the frozen, windswept Heath
for hours, returned, put on the washing, prepared my
breakfast, it's all ready for me, with the newspaper.

'Will you please HELP ME,' shouts Treasure. She
often needs help at just such a moment.

'I've done all this tidying and can you at least take
the cups down and bring me an empty dustbin. I need a
dustbin.' She is outraged that I am relaxing over breakfast while she toils away. She has stopped me in the nick
of time.

'Why don't you come downstairs and empty the

dustbin yourself?' I speak ever so calmly. This is my new policy of not screaming at Treasure. I mustn't over-react, say my advisers. I must remember that I'm the grown-up. I may only become agitated if life is endangered. If Treasure chooses to go out in a chiffon blouse with wet hair hanging in frozen spikes round her neck in February, she may do so. If she wishes to whistle incessantly, refuse breakfast and watch sex and violence on the telly, I mustn't shout. I must wait until something really serious happens.

I am not shouting. Treasure is. 'I've done all this tidying,' she shrieks again. 'I can't do everything. Look. Just look at my room. All you have to do is empty the bin.'

For the first time in living memory Treasure's carpet is visible in its entirety. Her clothes are neatly arranged in cupboards. She is wild with exhaustion, her hair sticking out. She can do no more. She is desperate for a takeover. 'Will you please hoover my room,' she commands. My inactivity is driving her over the edge.

'I will,' I say, 'but not this very minute.' And we are saved by the bell. The telephone rings, for once a timely distraction. I empty the bin. This may sound like kowtowing to a despot, but Treasure's efforts have been stunning compared to past tidyings. Only last month Lodger sneered at her housework. I had asked her to bring her dirty crockery out of the living room. I imagined it might reach the kitchen but Treasure managed to get it only as far as the hall carpet, just outside the living room door, where Lodger spotted it.

'Look,' he gloated. 'Look where she's put it.' He is thrilled to bits because *his* children take things regularly to the sink and even wash them up. But their mummy is immaculate and Treasure's isn't. I have set her rather a poor example in the past. Now, probably too late, I am making huge efforts to tidy. Perhaps my example is catching on.

Treasure has thrown away mountains of rubble. Usually I cannot get her to part with anything. 'What about this?' I have asked, holding up an ancient limb of Sindy doll.

'No,' Treasure has wept. 'I want to keep it.' But now a ton of mementoes has been cast aside. What can be goading her on? She seems to be under tremendous pressure. Together we complete the final hoovering, picking up any specks that might upset and deactivate our sensitive hoover.

The doorbell rings. It is Rosie and Lizzie. They are to stay the night. Just in time Treasure's pigsty has been turned into a palace fit to receive these sophisticates. Perhaps there are advantages to peer pressure.

Grandpa's tidying

Grandpa has always tidied in rather an aggressive way using naval epithets. 'Clear the decks,' he will snap, as if to galley slaves. 'Drink this up,' he shouts. 'Drink it,' pointing to a cup of warm tea. He is desperate to whisk it away but he cannot allow the beverage to be wasted.

In a recent frenzy of tidying he has swept away Grandma's false teeth. She left them on a kitchen surface for a moment and before she knew it they'd disappeared without trace. She flounced off to bridge in a fury leaving orders that Grandpa search the bag of rubbish. He grovelled away in it and found them, right at the bottom.

'Bloody idiot,' shouts Grandma upon her return. Grandpa is not a successful male role model at present. He feels unappreciated.

'I'm just a cabin boy,' he says, washing up and wiping surfaces. 'That's all I am. A cabin boy.' He has begun to brush his beard forward at the sides and tweak it into points in rather a stylish way, he feels, but Grandma finds it repulsive.

Treasure the hostess

Treasure has learned nothing from her experience of uncontrollable visitors. Our house seems to have become the pre-Strobe gathering place. It starts filling up at 6.30 p.m. Treasure has obviously informed the world that they may call here en route, have a light evening snack, clog up the living room and then escort her to the Strobe.

I open the door to several very large and unfamiliar youths.

'Yes?' I glare.

They glare back in a sullen way. I hear a polite voice from the back. It is Andrew, a recognisable member of the gang. These are his friends. I allow them in. I have planned to go out to dinner while Treasure has Rosie over for a quiet evening in, but the house is now packed with strange fellows and Treasure's plans seem rather fluid. She is keen for me to leave.

'When are you going out?'

'Soon. Will you please double-lock the back door?'

'Yes, yes.' She pokes her fingers into her ears in the usual way. Can I safely go out? Will our home be wrecked in my absence? Perhaps I should stay in supervising every weekend, fighting off gatecrashers and double-locking doors. I shall be Miss Havisham, at home in my decaying wedding dress, living vicariously through Treasure as she goes flouncing out into the world.

I make my escort review the scene of horror in the living room before we leave. He is unperturbed. He notices the dispersal pattern: boys to the left in a pile on the sofa, girls in a cluster on the right. 'They look alright to me.'

But I am thinking of the future. Every Saturday the crowds will grow, alien youths will pour into the house, the living room will be under occupation and I shall have nowhere to watch *Casualty*. I speak firmly to Treasure the next day.

'We can't have this every Saturday.'

'We're not going to,' barks Treasure, 'and I didn't know they were all coming. They all went by nine thirty.' She is outraged by my complaint. 'I *made* them go. What is your problem?' She can deal with rampaging youths. Easy. But what chills her to the marrow is the threat of a hovering mother.

'Just tell them not to do that next week.' My Saturday nights are obviously down the pan. I must in future be on guard duty. Following the fish murders, I am concerned about the dog's safety and my sofa, purchased recently and still spotless.

I greet next Saturday's hordes fiercely, wrenching the front door open and glaring. They are ever so polite. 'I'm Mark,' says one in a disarming way, offering a hand for me to shake.

'I'm David,' says another, smiling sweetly. I point sternly to the Treasure's room. They swarm upstairs. This time I bagsy the living room. Treasure packs the visitors into her boudoir – nine large boys and five large

81

girls, but this time their visit is brief – only half an hour before the exodus to the Strobe. Things are looking up. I remain on duty ready to expel miscreants, but there are none. Perhaps I have been too harsh. They troop off looking harmless and their manners are impeccable. One of them escorts Treasure home from the Strobe on the dot of midnight, just as he promised.

'See,' he says. 'I said I'd bring her home.'

Treasure is not even scowling.

'Did you have a lovely time?'

'Yes,' says she, glowing with happiness. 'I chipped my front tooth on a bottle and Rosie burnt her cheek on a cigarette.'

Nightmare on Oxford Street

Treasure has entered paradise. She is in Miss Selfridge with a fat wadge of birthday money. She flits from rack to rack, soon acquiring an armful of garments. Bits trail on the floor, hangers fall off. Treasure begins to panic. Drowning in clothes, she calls for assistance.

'Help me. I can't hold this. Can you please just take something.' It is obviously my fault that she is overloaded. I assist her. I trail behind, laden with the selection. My legs ache. They ached as soon as I saw Selfridges. I long to sit on the floor. Throbbing pop music belts through the shop.

We stagger to the changing rooms where Treasure tries on numerous ribbed and clinging tops and some black worm dresses in slithery fabrics. She is seized with embarrassment in mass changing rooms and so very vulnerable to criticism.

'Do you like it?' she asks. This is an order.

'Yes. Very nice. Lovely.' I mustn't say no. I can say 'Lovely but you've already got one', but I can't express an opinion or point out any flaws. Enviously I watch the woman next to us with her daughter. The daughter is also trying on skin-tight worm clothes, but short ones.

'It suits you from the back,' says the mummy strictly, 'but not from the front.' And the daughter is still smiling. Why can't Treasure respond in such a reasonable way? She has put on a long black worm down to her ankles and is scowling.

'What do you think?' She glares at the mirror.

'I don't really like the material.' Treasure is enraged. 'It makes you look very thin.' She perks up. 'Too thin,' I say. She is thrilled.

'I love it,' says Treasure. She spots my face. 'You don't like it. What's the matter with it?'

I point out an ill-fitting area around the middle. Treasure rips it off in a bate and tries on another one – a long black 100% nylon worm again but this time with long sleeves. She adores it. It exaggerates her wasp waist and enlarges her bosom. Rapture. She must have it. A terrifying choice.

'Like it?' There is a hint of threat in her voice.

'Very nice but where will you wear it?' She could have sung happy birthday to President Kennedy in it.

'Lots of places.' Treasure changes tactics. 'Please say you like it.' She is desperate for this frock. I am desperate to get out. Treasure buys it, plus some worm tops.

On to Hennes. Treasure selects some red tartan skirts, a rather demure length. She looks perfect. I experience a brief moment of hope but she rejects them and buys another ribbed worm top.

Time is running out. Treasure must be home by six because it is Saturday and she has made complex arrangements. We have only dealt with a fraction of

Oxford Street. And then I spot a dream top for me. Right colour, shape and size. For years I have searched for just such a garment. I stop to purchase it.

Treasure is incensed. We haven't done Next, Kookaï, Warehouse or Top Shop yet. She is white with panic. 'I can't wait,' she snaps. 'I'm going.' She stamps off, out into the milling crowds, leaving me stuck at the till. I want my garment. But how will Treasure get home? How will she find the car? Will I ever see her again? Yes. There is her little face, pale and agitated, at the entrance. She returns and stands behind me, limp with despair. Time is running out.

We have a small fight on the pavement. 'This is MY birthday shopping day / I want ten minutes of it / I hate you / You're selfish / You spoil everything.' Teeth clenched, sweating, we race around a few more shops and back to the car. It is over.

My neighbour Mrs Perez also went shopping today. She said she heard similar squabbles up and down Oxford Street. Perhaps there is a chance that Treasure and I are just normal pre-Christmas shoppers.

Beginning of the clothes problem

I noticed the Serious Clothes Problem some time ago. Treasure was twelve, coming on thirteen. She was just embarking on the flouncing, sneering, head-tossing, hair-flipping, excessive telephoning stage. I had perhaps foolishly allowed her to go shopping with her own pocket money and a seemingly sensible older friend, to buy clothes in the Holloway Road, expecting her to return with a T-shirt or leggings – something innocent and befitting a twelve-year-old.

She returned instead with a black number – high neck, cutaway shoulders, in skin-tight lycra and just covering her bum. Perfect for a nineteen-year-old vamp.

'Everyone needs a black number,' said she strictly.

She put on dangly earrings, piled her hair up fetchingly and bopped in front of the mirror, admired by the friend. 'Isn't it lovely? Daisy likes it, don't you Daisy?'

Lucky Daisy's mother. Her daughter was the adviser, not the purchaser. Treasure has long legs, long hair, the beginnings of a figure and looks lovely. I am keen to tell her that she may never wear the dress in public unless handcuffed to my wrist. Better still, I could order her to take it back to the shop.

'Very nice,' say I weedily, 'but rather grown-up.' Anything to avoid the word 'sexy'. And no, she may not wear it to the Holloway Odeon on a Saturday night.

I ask advice. Opinions are numerous, very forth-coming and rather contradictory: Treasure knows perfectly well what she's doing; she doesn't know what she's doing; don't allow it; let her wear it, they all wear things like that now; don't worry, nothing will happen; everything will happen; make her wear thick black tights; repress her now and she'll rebel later; now's the time to clamp down, because soon you won't be able to. Meanwhile Treasure is emulating Madonna. She apparently senses no danger.

This is worse than the Great Trainer Debate and the Can-I-have-a-Chipie-T-shirt. That was all easy. I forbade Nike Air and Chipie garments – obvious rip-off, immoral, materialistic – and she could sulk all she liked, I wasn't buying any. But this is about sex. I remember myself at this stage, stooping and skulking around in large black jumpers to conceal any hint of female shape, too embar-rassed to dance and wanting a nose-job and a wig. The complete opposite of Treasure. She seems to be doing rather better than I did. I would hate to crush her confidence.

The black dress problem solved itself in the end. Treasure noticed after a few days of prancing in it before the mirror, that if she were to bend over only two degrees her knickers would show. She put on tights voluntarily, wore a gargantuan T-shirt over the dress concealing all but the neck, discarded the earrings, scrunched her hair into a knot and went to the disco looking almost frumpish. A relief for me but only temporary.

The dress problem soon reared its head again on our Greek island holiday. Treasure spotted another dress, striped this time, with short sleeves, a rather low neck, in skin-tight lycra and just below the bum again. She'd been promised a summer dress, she didn't have one and this was her choice. We couldn't find the sort of dress that I'd expected; nothing ethnic and demure in embroidered white cotton. This island was up to date. It provided ouzo-friendly T-shirts, fluorescent lilos, very rude post cards and models of bonking turtles.

I allowed the dress and accompanied Treasure everywhere. The Greeks behaved impeccably. They took no notice, they were busy working. Only the English sniffed disapprovingly. One single radical approved. It was society's problem, said she, not Treasure's. It was what others saw in it, not what the child meant. And anyway, I wasn't keen to issue dire warnings about Humbert Humberts, date rape, Aids, pregnancy and condoms to someone of twelve.

I tried a warning.

'You think I look horrid,' sobbed Treasure.

No, I told her, she looked lovely, but she looked nineteen and people might treat her accordingly. What did she think of that?

She didn't know or care about it. She quoted Madonna. Madonna dresses to please herself. So perhaps I should have banned the video and the films and the TV programmes and the teen magazines.

Back home Treasure was safe in her school uniform. The trouble was that the skirt looked rather short. I suspected Treasure had been rolling the waistband over. The dress problem was obviously here for good.

The two faces of Treasure

Treasure comes home from school looking cheery. There, for a brief second in the doorway, is a happy face, a smiling schoolgirl home for tea. Emboldened, I ask a question.

'Had a nice day?' In a flash Treasure's expression changes. It becomes thunderous. She has remembered that she must not be pleasant to her mother. She dredges up a minor misdemeanour.

'You didn't give me my money for the school trip. I had to borrow some.' She sweeps past, hurls her bag to the floor and stamps up the stairs grumbling fiercely. 'Other mothers remember to give their children money.' She enters the bathroom. Slam.

'What trip?' Treasure turns the taps full on to hamper our conversation. I know nothing of a school trip. Treasure likes to keep them a secret. I am never given the tiniest smidgen of information in advance. Apparently Treasure never receives forms. Others do but she doesn't. She swears it.

This is a rough week for us anyway. Grandpa is suddenly whisked into hospital and Grandma, weakened by a nine-hour wait in a transit ward by his side, is ill at home in Brighton. I must go and visit, leaving Treasure alone with the neighbour, the lodger and the dog. There are numerous instructions that I need to impart before I leave. Treasure is desperate not to hear them.

'Please double-lock the back door.'

'Alright, alright,' Treasure screams, waving her arms about.

'With this key.'

'I know, I know.' She doesn't know. For some reason she refuses to look at the key. A burglar will find it before she does.

'Look. It's here. Just look at it.'

'Leave me alone.' Treasure is frenzied. She jams her fingers into her ears and runs bellowing from the kitchen. I now cannot demonstrate the dog's dinner measuring cup or the snacks and clothes for school tomorrow. All attempts at information drive Treasure to the brink of madness.

I leave her in a state of ignorance, shut in her room and insulated by roaring pop music. I ring my neighbour later to check. Everything is fine, says she. Treasure is calm and inoffensive and doing her homework. I check again in the morning with Lodger.

'It's all sweetness and light here,' says he smugly. Treasure is up, dressed and eating breakfast. She is not late and screaming in the usual way.

Tonight she is to travel to Brighton, alone for the first time on a Big Train. There are those who sneer, but I feel that Victoria mainline station may be something of an ordeal, so I employ Mrs Perez's daughter as an escort. I ring Treasure with instructions.

91

'Will you please tell Caroline . . .'

'I'm going. I'm late. GOODBYE.' Treasure shouts wildly, threatening to slam the phone down.

'Stop,' I scream. 'Listen to me. Wait. Tell Caroline to ring and tell me which train you're on.'

'Goodbye,' roars Treasure. Grandma is further weakened by terror. She knows for certain that of all the thousands of commuters on Network Southeast, it is *her* grandchild who will be snatched and murdered by a madman. Waiting later at the station I have caught Grandma's panic. What if Treasure does not appear? Crowds pour from the train. No Treasure. Something nasty is happening to my stomach. And just as I plan my call to the police, Treasure appears. Smiling. She is thrilled with her achievement and quite forgets to be horrid all evening. Travelling alone is now her passion. She had efficiently packed a picnic and can't wait to travel home alone again tomorrow.

Imagine her disappointment on learning that I, her odious mother, am to drive her home with me.

'No, no. You're not to come.' Treasure is in despair again. 'Why do you always have to spoil everything?'

Treasure changes her mind

Treasure has had a relaxing couple of weeks, suspiciously free of homework. She is bike riding, visiting, bopping and lolling about like mad. What can be going on?

'No homework today?' I ask repeatedly.

'No,' says Treasure airily, prancing about the house. But the truth will out. One day she slips up and mentions exams. They are now only one week away. Treasure should have been revising. The magical thing about revision, she has found, is that it doesn't have to be handed in.

I impose a rigid timetable and carry out regular inspections, because she can pretend to be doing it. She can sit in her room surrounded by books but secretly trying on clothes and make-up, or she can can study *Just 17* and call it Media Studies.

Treasure is to stay in and work. She may not leave the house until several hours of revision have been done. She retires grumpily to her room. It is Saturday and she has arranged to meet Andrew and Rosie at six. I have therefore arranged to go out at seven. Treasure has three hours left in which to revise. She endures half an hour, then bursts from her room as if from Rampton. She cannot be restrained.

'I've got to go to the library,' says she with a hunted look.

'You haven't time,' I say. 'It's not worth it.' The library is half an hour away. 'If you're going to meet everyone at six then you'd better stay here.'

'I'm not going to meet them,' says Treasure. 'I'm not going out till nine. I'm only going to the Strobe.'

As Treasure now has aeons of time, I agree to take her to the library. This change of plan has made a hash of my evening. It means that Treasure will be alone at the house pre-Strobe at risk of gatecrashers. It is now too late to hire a childminder/security guard. I must make complex arrangements with neighbours to be on the alert. Treasure is rather sullen in the car.

'What's the matter?'

'You won't let me go to Rosie or Andrew's house. I wasn't allowed to meet them.'

I am stunned by Treasure's mendacity. I said nothing of the kind. I shout. 'I WANTED you to go out at six.'

'Stop the car,' shrieks Treasure. 'Stop. I don't want to go to the library.'

'You're not bloody going to the library.' I drive wildly round the block. 'You can stay at home and go out at six as planned.' I deposit Treasure at the end of the road. 'I am going shopping,' I say. 'GET ON WITH YOUR WORK.'

'I can't work here,' screams Treasure. 'I can work better in the library with all the right books around me.'

There are often revising boys around the library. She is now tense and pale. The spectre of exams looms. Still she procrastinates. Still the loud background music, the Strobe, the friends, the telephone calls, the endless bus journeys and lifts to the library are an absolute must. She cannot bear to give up one scrap of anything. The word sacrifice is anathema to Treasure.

'Go home and DO SOME WORK,' I scream, 'or you won't be going anywhere.'

Treasure looks baffled. She cannot for the life of her understand my behaviour. She has done as she is told. There she is, ready to revise. She is doing it at home as ordered.

'Why are you cross with me?' asks Treasure. 'You're always cross with me.'

Treasure talks of boyfriends

Treasure and I are driving along the High Street past a trio of pallid youths. 'Oh my God,' trills Treasure. 'Look. It's Barry Tate. It's Lizzie's last boyfriend.' She indicates the one with a ponytail and partially shaven head.

'I must tell Lizzie. She won't believe it. I went out with him before her.'

This is news to me. I cannot recall the name Tate or any outings without the gang. I ask for clarification. 'What do you mean, "went out"?'

Treasure is in an instant fury. 'Just shut up Mummy.' Her excitement is poisoned by my enquiry. 'You're so stupid.'

I persist rashly. 'But where do you go?'

Treasure can tolerate no more. 'Why do you ask that? Other mothers don't. They just say "Oh how nice." Why can't you do that?'

We drive on in a tense way. I may have been nosy but at least I didn't criticise Treasure's choice. She, however, criticises mine and enquires like anything.

'Why does He keep phoning up?' she asks with a

knowing sneer. 'Is He your boyfriend?' It is difficult for me to say yes with confidence.

'He's just a friend of mine,' say I primly.

Spotting him one day in the kitchen, Treasure twirls in for a proper look. She has suddenly become a keen sandwich and tea maker and devoted dog owner, determined to brush and feed the dog. It all keeps her busy in the kitchen forever, slightly flushed and trying not to smirk. And all this at a time when she is usually sunk in front of the telly absorbing soaps. She now cannot choose between us and *Home and Away*.

'He's gross,' says she later, rather bluntly. 'Yuk. He's so fat. Can't you find someone better looking?' She looks at me with pity. Not only is she repelled by my choice, but realises that it sometimes impedes her use of the telephone. Yet another person is blocking up the line. She becomes immensely suspicious and keen to follow the plot of my romance.

'Who do you think's going to phone?' she asks in a withering way. 'Is He going to phone?' She never imagines it might just be Grandma with the latest on *Coronation Street* or the merits of Fybogel. She will loiter, earwigging while I speak, or will flounce and argue when asked to leave the room. She has recently taken particular exception to him since he rang and suggested she fetch her mother at once. Treasure isn't keen on brisk instructions. She now answers his calls frostily, dangling the phone from its cord at arm's length, her face wrinkled with distaste.

'It's Him.'

Seconds before I leave for my date, a mysterious and lightning illness will often strike Treasure down.

'I'm ill,' she shouts, her vocal cords the only part of her body that retain any strength. Pasty and dishevelled in her nightie, she staggers to the door as I leave. 'How can you go out? You don't care. When it comes down to it, who do you choose? You choose HIM.'

I leave the house accursed, my sick daughter alone with the dog and the babysitter. Her last minute desperate calls for lemon and honey, paracetamol and a kiss have made me late. The effect of my perfumed and relaxing bath is ruined. Guilt and haste have altered my complexion. I go out with a corned-beef face.

Meanwhile Treasure's social life is flourishing. Boyfriends ring by the dozen and call by in droves. I still don't know what 'going out' means. I've wondered for years. Treasure often mentioned it in her youth, when she never went out unsupervised. She could 'go out' without going out. She still can. But things are changing. The horse pictures and dog frieze that used to adorn her bedroom have been replaced by pictures and photos of chaps. No sign of Barry Tate though. No one with a shaved head. Yet.

Treasure asks too much

This week it is Treasure's turn to entertain the gang at our house.

'Can Andrew stay the night if he can't get home?'

'Yes,' I say. 'He can sleep on the sofa.'

Treasure is flabbergasted. 'What? Why the sofa?' she asks, her eyes open wide, her jaw dropping open. She is all innocence.

'Well he can't sleep in your room.'

'Why not? What's the matter with you?' Treasure stares at me in a puzzled way.

She wants it spelled out. 'You can't have a boy sleeping in your room.'

'What?' Treasure throws herself about the sofa, laughing wildly and kicking her legs in the air. She sits up again. 'You're not serious. I can't believe what I'm hearing. You're so Victorian.' She continues to roll about the sofa, laughing in a loud and mocking way.

'What do you think we'll do?' she sneers. 'We're just friends. We always sleep together.' Treasure imparts this devastating news two minutes before my departure to the cinema. I am leaving her at the top of the slippery slope to ruin. 'Well you're not doing it here,' I snap. 'I shall speak to Andrew's parents.'

'Speak to them,' says Treasure icily. Her mockery has turned to disgust; her purity has been sullied by my filthy mind.

I return from the cinema to find Treasure calm, benign and alone, watching the telly in her nightie. She has just been escorted home by her friends after an evening at Richard's house watching TV with his mother. All very innocuous, but this is only a temporary reprieve. Treasure announces terrifying plans for the New Year. Rosie has invited her to spend several days in her father's cottage in Norfolk.

'She's going to invite eighteen,' says Treasure, thrilled to the marrow. 'That's how many can sleep. Her dad's letting her and he's not going to be there.'

Is the man out of his mind? Treasure must have got it wrong. But no. Rosie confirms it. 'We're going from the 2nd to the 7th,' says she, hugging Treasure and both jumping up and down on the front porch.

'How lovely,' say I, still convinced that this is a fantasy. What sensible grown-up would allow eighteen fourteen- to sixteen-year-olds of mixed gender to stay unsupervised for several days in his home? I decide not to panic until the plans are verified. Anyway, Treasure has more immediate plans for me to flap over – a holiday sleepover party to celebrate the end of exams. A mixed dormitory in our house is now her aim in life.

I ring Andrew's mother. What does she think? She thinks it's fine. Entirely innocent. She is laid back and liberal about it, but her child is male and aged fifteen and a half. I try Chloe's parents. No boy is allowed to stay overnight in their house, ever, says the daddy. Not so liberal. I carry out an opinion poll of neighbours. It is inconclusive. Separate them and they only fib and creep about in the night. Be repressive and they go elsewhere. Be too permissive and they are contemptuous.

I consider the mixed dormitories of my youth (youth meaning sixteen to twenty-one), on the way back from Aldermaston and at home with the parents away. There was very little drink, no sex to speak of and no drugs. For years. Someone was once sick up the hall wallpaper. But the age of innocence seems to zip past earlier and rather sharpish nowadays.

Assuming that it is still with us, I allow Treasure's sleepover – one boy and five girls in the living room, one depressed boy isolated upstairs. (He still has exams and must rest.) I look in in the morning. Downstairs resembles a youth hostel and locusts have swept through the chocolate biscuit tins. That's all I know.

Treasure's good report

It is parents' evening, usually a rather harrowing experience for me, but tonight is different. All teachers inform me that Treasure's behaviour has improved no end. She is now a calm and pleasant child. Two large works of Treasure's art are on display in the entrance hall. Teachers ask me what has happened. Nothing that I am aware of. Life at home continues in much the same grisly way. But at school Treasure has become a shadow of her former pesky self.

There is only one small worry expressed. Is she there at all? Sometimes she seems to be in something of a dream, say the odd one or two teachers. Perhaps she is there in body but in spirit she is off at the Strobe, bopping and stage-diving and wheedling free orange juice out of the favourite bouncer.

Her social life is too thrilling for words at present. It perhaps floats into her mind and obliterates past participles, quadratic equations and the digestive system. It rather blots out academic life at home. Treasure cannot study in a quiet, peaceful way. She is a caged beast, pacified only by loud music, screeching, telephoning, hair-washing and bathing. She is in and out like a yo-yo, as if repelled by the interior of our house. She feels it is her duty to go out, stay out and not sleep at weekends, leaving no time or strength for homework.

I have therefore made a rule that Treasure may only have one late night at weekends. She tries to ignore this rule. Friday, I am driving her to Chloe's house and she reveals her plans in the car. Tomorrow she is going to the Strobe and Sunday to Andrew's house.

'You may not go out at all on Sunday.'

'Why not? I told you weeks ago I was going. How can you be so mean?' Treasure flicks on Kiss PM. It is raining, we are jammed in the Friday night traffic.

'Turn that down. You're not even meant to be out tonight.'

'I must go.' Treasure is at breaking point. 'I promised. I haven't seen Chloe for weeks. And I must see Andrew. He invited me.'

'Not a chance in hell,' I shout.

Treasure screams abuse in the usual way and flicks to Capital. I wonder why I am driving her anywhere. Infuriated by Capital, Treasure's offensive epithets and my own inability to apply rules, I begin a suicidal U-turn in the Holloway Road.

'What are you doing?' screams Treasure. 'You're mad.' She is right. Where will it get me? Traffic stretches chock-a-block for miles both ways. I cannot go back, the rain beats down, Treasure weeps. 'Please don't,' she begs. 'Please take me to Chloe's.'

All around motorists are bibbing, roaring and gesturing crudely. They are thrilled to have spotted yet

103

another faulty woman driver to mock. I reverse my U-turn. I am screaming, Treasure is sobbing. We continue. I stab fiercely at the Radio 3 button. Horrid Aaron Copeland – the last thing on earth I want to hear. I stab Radio 4. Treasure dare not speak or poke radio buttons. My wild driving has silenced her.

We arrive at Chloe's both pale and shaking. Treasure and Chloe are to go to bed at ten thirty. No one dares to argue. I return to the car to cry.

Remembering this and similar events, the parents' evening report comes as rather a shock.

'Tell me what they said,' Treasure asks the minute I return. 'Tell me everything.' I tell. Treasure feels that a reward is in order.

'Now I've been so good I want to ask you a favour. Can I go and see Impetigo playing at Leicester Square? Please please. It finishes at 4 a.m. and I've bought my ticket.'

'No you can't.'

'But it's in my holidays.' Treasure is astounded again. 'And I've been so good. I do everything I'm told, I'm never late, I always ring and tell you where I am and you're STILL horrid to me.'

Winter

No snow this winter, rather disappointingly, but it was only trouble when we did have it. It emphasised the terrible social divide along our street. There were Mrs Perez and I and Treasure and the perfect boy and the Rodrigo girls getting ready to go tobogganing on the Heath, but we didn't have the proper equipment. Some of our gloves were ill-matched and our anoraks weren't all properly waterproof and we only had tea-trays and polythene bags to slide on.

We were all getting into the car in a cheery way when the people on the other side of the road came out with the same intentions. But they had lovely wooden sledges and smart matching mittens, scarves and hats, and daddies in bobble-hats to provide a decent role model. *And* they had south-facing gardens.

It all plunged Mrs Perez into a gloom and feelings of inadequacy. *Her* husband was chain smoking in the living room reading a Wordsworth biography, curtains drawn, not a chink of winter sun allowed in. If only he were to put on a bobble-hat and dash about in the snow getting involved. Mrs Perez has given up all hope really.

Still, the Heath was magic and sparkly in the frost and snow with the slanty sun coming down. The dog was over-excited by it all. It belted round in enormous circles at a furious speed. Apparently the frost makes everything smell even more thrilling, if you are a dog.

It was heaven for all of us for about twenty minutes, until everybody's gloves got wet and Treasure's fingers got cold and mine went white and numb. We came home frozen and weeping with discomfort. I bet that over the road there was no snivelling. I bet they all took thermoses full of boiling hot choc and came home cheerful and glowing. Mrs Perez and I didn't look. We were trying to warm everyone up, but that is our fantasy. It is based on careful observation.

I reminded Mrs P that in our back gardens, due to the lack of sun, the snowmen do last much longer. This winter has been far less enervating.

Treasure's seasonal dilemma

Treasure and I are fighting and squeezing our way through the packed and crabby hordes, Christmas shopping in town. This is Treasure's favourite place to be. She is keen to spend large amounts of saved up pocket money on presents. We are on the last leg of our outing. She only has one more present to find, one for me, when we see the poor man.

He looks very poor – an old, pale, sick and raggedy version of Grandpa. His nose is dripping and he's holding a very few boxes of matches in his trembly fingers.

Treasure wants to give him some money. We both give him some. Cynics might say that he has a secret suite at the Curzon, but Treasure and I are convinced that he is utterly wretched.

'We should have given him more.' Treasure enters Marks and Spencers in despair. 'Why didn't you give him more than that? Go back again.'

'He'll still be there when we come out.'

But Treasure's outing is ruined. She stamps round the store in a towering rage. 'It's disgusting,' she snaps.

'Look at that woman in a fur coat.' Her voice rises in a menacing way, disturbing nearby shoppers. 'What a waste of money.' Treasure has become a socialist.

'I hate it here,' she shouts on the escalator. 'Look at them. Look at all that stuff they've bought. I'm not getting anything else. I want to give it to that man instead.'

'Good idea,' I say. 'That's very kind of you.'

'What about your present?'

'I've got enough presents.' I am delighted by Treasure's altruism and to have the shopping curtailed. We battle our way through the mass of vile capitalist shoppers and out into the street. Will he still be there? We are on tenterhooks. Yes. There he is, white and shaky, holding out the dreaded matchboxes. Treasure rushes over and stuffs all her money into his hands. He drops a few matchboxes. Treasure picks them up.

She feels rather odd on the way home. She needs to phone, visit and dash about. She wants to talk to someone sensitive. She rushes to Lizzie's house to tell her about the man while I have a relaxing tea-break. Ten minutes later there is wild ringing at the doorbell. It is Treasure, distraught again.

'I hate her. Horrid cow. I hate her.' Treasure hurls herself on to the sofa and sobs hopelessly.

'What's the matter? What's she said?'

'She said I'm stupid,' howls Treasure. 'I told her about that man and she said "People like that should be dead".' I am horrified by Lizzie's callous response, but Treasure is tormented by horrible doubts. 'I'm so stupid. Why did I do that? I shouldn't have done it.'

'Yes you should. It was very kind of you.' Treasure is

not convinced. I try harder, describing her action and personality in glowing terms, but she doesn't believe me. How galling to find that all my powers of persuasion are as nought when pitted against one throwaway comment, even a fascist comment, from a chum. This must be peer pressure.

Treasure will not be comforted. She never wants to speak to Lizzie again. She plans to run soup kitchens throughout the holidays and devote every spare minute of her time to the homeless and rootless. I am to go with her. The immediate future looks grim.

I mention the poor man to Grandpa. He does mocking imitations with a box of matches, fortunately in Treasure's absence. I order him *never* to do that in her presence. How will Treasure manage? It's not just sex, drugs, exams and inner-city violence. Now she's up against the obstacles to idealism.

Treasure the romantic

Treasure is rather preoccupied by romance at present – her own and everyone else's. I hear riveting snippets of her telephone chats: so-and-so is going, is not going, wants to, does not want to go out, with so-and-so. I am not allowed to discuss this topic. Sometimes I am given a smidgen of information, an edited version: 'Rosie is going to dump Andrew,' but I may not comment.

The noxious word 'snogging' has entered Treasure's vocabulary. Relatively innocuous itself, it presumably heralds the advent of sex, about which Treasure prattles non-stop to her chums. I may not participate in these discussions or pass an opinion because it is clear to Treasure that I know nothing about it and she knows everything.

She lives in a frank new world where information and free condoms are liberally showered upon her. She knows about venereal disease, deviants, bizarre sexual proclivities, abortions, miscarriages, lovebites and blow-jobs. I find this rather depressing. It is not the sort of knowledge with which I want her mind to be stuffed.

Treasure takes it in her stride. She seems unperturbed by all this grisly information. She gathers it wherever she goes – from her friends, her magazines, the Strobe. The Strobe kindly gave an Aids and condom information evening last week. Treasure and Rosie had a thrilling time filling condoms with water and bursting them over chums. Treasure inadvertently splashed someone bad-tempered who nearly kicked her head in and had to be restrained, but she and Rosie still came bouncing home cheerily, stocked up with free condoms. Apparently Treasure now has a secret store in her bedroom.

I cannot help but compare this with my own youth, when Jennifer Wickenden, aged fourteen, came into school one day and told us that her sister had got married and said that Doing It was nice. We were all shocked to the marrow. But here is Treasure, plunged into an underworld of drugs, sex and violence and relatively unruffled.

I notice, while supply teaching in the inner city, that sex education is awfully frank nowadays. We had a condom demonstration for ten- to eleven-years-olds the other day. Teacher held up a condom and stretched and pinged it and blew it up like a balloon in a trendy, carefree way. Nobody laughed. 'What other barrier methods are there?' asked Teacher. Pupils answered obediently. They got a little muddled over intra-uterine devices.

'Repeat after me,' said Teacher strictly, bellowing each word separately. Returning to condoms, a rather perky child spoke up.

'Please Miss,' said she, 'you can get them with a feather on the end.'

'No you can't,' said Teacher, fibbing crossly.

111

'Yes you can Miss. I saw it in a book.' I am keen to know which book, but as a supply teacher I must take a back seat in these discussions.

'No you can't.' Teacher didn't seem eager to embark on this debate.

'Yes you can,' said a boy at the back, clear as a bell and with a ring of authority. 'It's for erotic pleasure.'

Even Teacher was silenced, and she was a bold woman. She had already festooned the classroom with menstrual charts, sanitary towel and tampon displays, detailed life-sized drawings of genitalia and long lists of Words We Use At Home – a selection of rather crude names of parts and physical functions.

Later, in came Mrs S, a parent. 'WE don't use those words at home,' said she, her chin wrinkled with distaste. 'Neither do we,' said I, ganging up treacherously.

Luckily Treasure's school is less progressive. They've started with flowers and now they're doing rabbits. I am rather relieved. If Treasure has to live in the modern world, at least she can have a breather from it sometimes. She can wear her uniform and learn about rabbits, just for a couple more years.

A dangerous evening

I have left Treasure alone on a Saturday night awaiting Rosie while I go to the theatre. Treasure promises absolutely to be off the phone at seven fifteen so that I can ring and check her arrangements.

I ring at seven fifteen, pre-theatre. Engaged. I ring at eight forty-five, interval. Engaged. I find it difficult to relax. This is fringe theatre with much screaming and some nudity, all only three feet away. And what is Treasure doing?

I ring post-theatre, no answer. The little wretch has gone out. Where to? I have banned the Strobe because Treasure has been poorly all week. I cannot have a relaxing drink and snack with friends. I feel I must go home and investigate Treasure's whereabouts. I return to find the house empty. No notes, no clues. I ring all local friends. No Treasure. My stomach goes funny. I wander about the house, I run trembling to Mrs Perez and demand a cigarette. I decide, before I phone the police, to walk up the road with the dog and search the Strobe.

I start walking, thinking of female teenage murdered

corpses. I am beginning to gibber. I have been advised not to scream at Treasure when and if I find her.

As I approach the Strobe I see her running blithely across the road alone. This is the one thing she is absolutely forbidden to do – to go out by herself in the streets at night. It is eleven forty. Ignoring advice I scream at once. 'WHAT ARE YOU DOING?'

Treasure skips cheerily towards me. I shriek like a mad woman.

'How dare you be out here by yourself?'

'I can explain. Let me explain.' Treasure is remarkably self-contained in the presence of a foaming lunatic. 'My friends are at the station,' says she. 'I was just crossing the road to see them.' She insists that both sides of the road are clogged with friends and escorts. She was merely crossing from one group to another. She is as safe as houses.

I am still a demented creature. My throat is closing up. It cannot cope with my demands. I rush Treasure home. She battles on with her explanation. Thirty gate-crashers arrived, says she. They telephoned the world, they rushed into the street with her violin, they crowded into the kitchen and bathroom. Treasure ran to Jane the neighbour for help. Jane cleared them out in a flash. But overwhelmed by her ghastly experience, Treasure forgot her plan to stay in and felt an urgent need to visit friends at the station, forgetting to leave me a note.

'I'll never do it again,' she weeps.

'You bet you won't,' say I, cruel as ever. I ban next week's Impetigo concert. Treasure misinterprets my rage. She assumes that my crazed concern about her welfare implies dislike.

114

'You hate me,' sobs Treasure, and goes to bed in despair.

I wake up feeling ill and rather glum the next day. My throat has not quite recovered. General consensus from advisers is that proper, adequate grown-ups do not scream and shout. They control themselves. I am setting Treasure an atrocious example and training her to grow up a maniac in my image. I long to crawl into a cave and live as an anchorite for the next decade, but who would look after Treasure and the dog? They would feel abandoned, although a sensible replacement would be in their interest.

Luckily Mrs C up the road admits to screaming like a banshee at her children. I have always looked upon Mrs C as more than adequate. She and I compete for title of loudest screamer. I feel a little better. Also, Treasure spring-cleans the whole kitchen and bathroom voluntarily while I am out walking the dog.

Still, I am planning never to scream again – my new resolution. Treasure is not assisting me in my resolve. I begin to speak in a civilised tone at all times, even when issuing a reprimand, but Treasure pretends I am still shouting.

'Dinner's ready,' say I, polite as anything.

'Calm down, calm down,' yells the Treasure. She is obviously now programmed to high-decibel instructions. I breathe deeply and watch the dinner congeal and chill. How long till Treasure learns the new pattern? Will I last?

Treasure takes a bath

The dog and I have just returned from our daily trek over the Heath in sub-zero temperatures. I am in desperate need of a lovely hot bath. I announce that I am about to have one.

'No. You can't.' Treasure is panic-stricken. She has not bathed for two days and cannot last a minute longer. 'I've got to have one now,' she moans.

'Alright.' I give in. I am too weak to fight. 'Leave the water in.' Fiennes-like I trudge to the paper shop. But upon my return Treasure is still not bathing. Daisy has turned up. They are tremendously busy phoning and video-watching.

'What about your bath?'

'You have it first,' says Treasure generously.

Bliss. I prepare my bath. Radio and telephone, tea and toast at hand, blueberry bubbles, passion-fruit oil, banana shampoo, apricot facial scrub. Attracted by the scent of fruit salad the dog enters the bathroom for a sip of aromatic bathwater. I sink into the scented foam. Two beautiful silent minutes go by.

116

Then a fierce banging on the door. Treasure sticks her head in accompanied by a piercing northerly wind from the hall.

'How long will you be?' she glares, holding the door open wide.

'Half an hour.'

'What?' Treasure is astounded. 'You're so selfish. I've been waiting an hour already. Why do you have to be so long?' Her mind possibly addled by phoning and squealing, Treasure seems to have lost track of time.

'Shut the door or I'll be even longer.'

'I can't believe this.' Treasure is exasperated beyond measure. 'Will you please hurry up,' says she in a menacing way.

'No. Go away.' I have pandered long enough. Treasure slams the door and stamps to her room in a bate. I hear the distant throb of roaring pop music. My bubbles have gone, the bathroom chilled, the water grey. I pretend to relax. As my bath no longer looks inviting, I feel that Treasure would prefer a fresh one. Wrong again. Hearing the sound of disappearing bathwater Treasure bounds in a fury to the bathroom. She is ready to kill.

'Why did you do that?' she screams. 'You know it'll go cold.' Treasure is right. Two baths in a row is a dreadful risk. Although a large tank and every radiator in the house is filled with scalding water, it may magically turn to ice half-way through a second bath. These are nerve-racking moments for me. Will the water go cold? Will our day be plunged into hell? I test the water at regular intervals. I am on a knife edge. It seems to be continuing hot. Bravely I summon the Treasure.

'It's cold,' she lies. I scuttle to the kitchen, my only

wish to please the Princess of North London. Quickly I put the kettle on, boil it, scurry back to the bathroom with it and knock obediently at the door.

'What do you want?' roars the Treasure. 'Just leave me alone.' I deposit the kettle and hide in my bedroom. I am determined to relax. I breathe deeply and read my gripping novel in a purposeful way. I hear the bathroom door open. More roaring. Then Treasure discovers the kettle. Silence descends on the house.

Later that day Treasure and I meet on the stairs.

'Thank you for the kettle,' says Treasure. She goes a little pink. 'Would you like a cup of tea?'

The telephone: Part 2

Our telephone bill is £325. I do not find this amusing. Treasure apparently does. She finds the whole thing hugely entertaining. She ignores repeated requests and reasonable arguments to limit usage, and when I finally approach, maddened, screaming hoarsely, 'Get off the phone', she will smirk in a relaxed way into its mouth-piece.

'She wants me to get off the phone,' she drawls, cool as anything, moving it a tiny bit away from her ear and enabling her chum to hear the silly mother roaring in the background.

She is dicing with death. The dog knows. It is hiding under the kitchen table looking crumpled, but Treasure doesn't care. She will risk anything to use the phone. Returning home from even the briefest excursion she will dart to it, grab it and cradle it on her knee.

'Who can I phone?' she asks, staring wildly into the air. She strokes its little plastic body. 'I'll phone Lizzie.'

'No you won't. It isn't six yet.'

'I must. I've got to.' Treasure is desperate for her next

fix. Her addiction has worsened over the last six months. She waits till six. She is on hot coals. She cannot rest, work or eat. She stalks the house watching the clock, waiting, hoping that someone will ring her and break her vigil. At six she clamps herself to the telephone, talking and laughing fiercely. I could have heard every top-volume word from the bottom of the garden but Treasure is determined that I shall not listen.

'Shut the door,' she roars bossily as I leave the room. I refuse. I am carrying a mountain of dirty cups, plates, banana and orange skins and chewed yoghurt pots that she and the dog have discarded. I haven't a free hand. If I had one I wouldn't use it because I, like Treasure, dislike being ordered about, especially in such a tone.

I don't really want the door shut anyway. Once it's shut the dog cannot get in or out freely and starts to bark and scratch and when Treasure is on the phone she is unable to move and attend to the dog's needs. It can scratch its claws off and bark itself dumb, Treasure will not move a muscle. I am forced to return on such occasions and let it out myself.

'Why didn't you open the door?' I snap.

'I didn't hear,' says Treasure, looking hurt. 'Really I didn't.'

But she can hear the telephone, even on the quietest ring and hidden under my double duvet. Someone phones at 10 p.m., Treasure's supposed bedtime. 'She's asleep,' I growl. But she has heard its tiny muffled ring. She crawls exhausted from her bed.

'Who was it?' she croaks. She cannot sleep without this knowledge. She cannot sleep with it. She will lie awake wondering what vital snippet she has missed and planning tomorrow's return call. And there's the rub. Put them off today and the little toads will only ring back tomorrow. The return calls mount up, a cumulative effect. I know that tomorrow will also be a hell of ringing, shrieking, arguing and may end in violence. Grandma, among others, will be coming out in spots down in Hove trying to get through.

I have wrenched the phone from its socket, smacked it from her hand, fisticuffs have ensued and the solution seems no nearer. 'Get Treasure her own phone,' say the liberals. 'Tell her this is not acceptable,' say the cleverdicks, but at last Mrs Perez has come up with a possible answer. What about Treasure's own phone *but* for incoming calls only. Then they can all phone her on that and at least my line will be clear. All I'll have to worry about is when, behind her closed bedroom door and glued to her own telephone, will Treasure ever do her homework and go to sleep.

'She's only copying you,' says Mrs Perez cruelly. 'What do you do when you're upset? You run to the phone and tell everyone.' My fault again. Now we know who is responsible for the country's economic crisis. Mr Lamont's mother.

Treasure the rebel

Treasure is always on the lookout for a boundary. Then she can smash through it, rampage on to the next one and give that a good bashing. And if she can't get through that way, she'll squirm and wheedle her way through rather slyly.

Things became rather lax over the holidays. They had to be tightened up once school had started. Homework had to be done; bedtime, clothing, manners and language regulated. I am now enforcing boundaries like billy ho. Treasure fights them all.

But I have found one that works – call barring on the telephone. I dial a secret code and a lady's voice says twice ever so politely, 'Outgoing calls are barred.' Heaven. I can leave the house knowing that there is at least one boundary being efficiently enforced. I phone Treasure from work to check on her welfare. She is stunned by my action. This is her first day at home alone with the call barring and it has given her a nasty turn. She is in a white hot fury. She cannot phone out and cannot go out to phone in case she misses someone phoning in. She won't go out to phone on principle anyway. She wants to suffer properly.

'Why did you do this to me?' screeches Treasure. 'I hate you. I can't arrange anything. Tell Lodger the code.'

I can't. Luckily I can't remember it. Even if I weedily wanted to relent I couldn't. Treasure is stymied.

'Go out and arrange from a phone box.'

'No I won't.' Treasure turns monosyllabic with vexation. She grunts a few answers.

'Have you had any breakfast?'

'Grunt.'

'Have you done some homework?'

'Grunt.' She has two weapons: her body and her brain. She will neglect them both and the ignorant and enfeebled result will be my fault. And she has more clever tricks up her sleeve for bedtime. It's easy. Just as we reach the agreed time for lights out, she will make an outrageous demand.

'Put the light out please.'

'Can I just read to the end of this book / watch this programme / have some pasta / let the dog stay here?'

'No.'

'Why not? Just fifteen minutes more.' She has cleverly started a row. She stamps up and down stairs to the toilet. I have upset her and if she's upset she can't sleep. So she'll be awake for ages anyway then she won't be able to get up, she'll be late for school, she'll be too crabby and tired to concentrate, Teacher will issue a detention slip. My fault again. Treasure will lurch home itching for a fight.

Now and again I give up rather feebly. The battle becomes too exhausting. 'Do what you like,' I say.

Treasure is not pleased. 'You don't care,' says she miserably. 'You don't care about me.' Her life takes on an aimless quality. She can barely manage with or without boundaries. She is worn out with battling. The boundary smashing seems to have taken on a momentum of its own. Treasure is on automatic pilot – programmed to defy even the weeniest, most innocuous instruction.

She is desperate for a brief respite, but has been invited to an all-night rave. 'Don't tell me I can't go. Please. Just don't,' she warns me. 'Because then I'll want to.'

The blue room

Treasure is having her room decorated. It is to be dark blue – all dark blue: walls, ceiling, woodwork, blinds and even lampshade. I suggest that she may not be able to see, but Treasure knows better. 'Chloe's lampshade is dark blue. I'll just have a stronger lightbulb.'

She is determined to live in gloom and darkness. She has rejected her existing delightful lampshade, decorated with puffy clouds and rainbows, shaped like a hot air balloon with weeny furry koalas and squirrels clinging to the basket. She is now going for serious design.

I am also trying to perk up the rest of the house. Hoping to conceal its tattiness I cram it with more plants and buy a Moroccan rug. Treasure cannot abide it.

'Errr!' She recoils, horrified. 'It looks like sick. I can't eat in here.' She grabs her dinner and rushes back to the kitchen, leaving me alone with *EastEnders*.

She may be right. The rug, charmingly subtle in the shop, now seems to be a predominantly crude and vicious yellow. It also has a suspicious dark patch at one end. Treasure rings Grandma at once to tell tales.

I cannot withstand a combined attack from Treasure and Grandma. I return the rug and swap it for another. Treasure is not averse to this one but quickly grows to hate it as I attempt to limit spending in her boudoir.

'You're so mean. Just because you've completely wasted all our money on that nasty rug. My friends think it's disgusting.'

My friends like it. Mrs Perez likes it. I no longer know if I like it. I have lost confidence in my plans for the living room. The spider plants are aggressively rampant and partially obscure Grandma's paintings – early Ruislip primitives. We are a bit sixties by accident. What luck it is all the rage at present: only Treasure's room is to be an oasis of cool.

Lodger is in charge of decorating. A perfectionist, he refuses to just slap on some blue paint. Everything must be stripped, replastered, sanded and repapered first. Rigorous preparations begin, the house is in turmoil and Treasure is moved to the spare room, her possessions in plastic bags.

'I feel upset,' says she. 'I want to cry.' Her make-up, tapes, Strobe passcard and holiday homework are all hidden in the mountain of bags. She has lost the will to sort and detests the spare room. She prefers my room with television and stereo at hand. Waif-like, she pleads for asylum. 'Please can I sleep in your room? Please?'

She has a hot choc and moves in. I move to the spare room. How long can this go on? I am terrified that Lodger, having reduced Treasure's room to a shell, will suddenly be overwhelmed with work for the next six months and unable to finish the decorating. Treasure and I will be rootless.

She calls from my bed, a note of urgency in her voice. She has spotted a special offer in her magazine – a black halter-neck dress for the summer. I recommend the white version but Treasure is not keen. She prefers to dress in black in her blue room courting depression.

Desperate to bring a scrap of sparkling colour into Treasure's deathly environment I suggest she decorates her furniture in an uplifting way. Varnished collage, perhaps, like Rosie's mother's Victorian screen.

'Don't be ridiculous,' she snarls. 'Leave it out.' A new sour note has entered her voice. She is weary of the world and my naive little suggestions. The blue paint is working already. From its tin.

Treasure helps with the decorating

The decorating is ruining Treasure's life. She is lost without her room and becomes crabbier by the day. She roams the house searching for a refuge from which she can ban her pestilential mother. Nowhere will do.

'Use the living room,' I say.

'You'll come in,' shouts Treasure. 'You'll want to watch telly.'

'No I won't.'

'Yes you will. You're here now. Just go away.' She is enraged by my suggestion that were she to help, the decorating might progress more quickly. Meanwhile Lodger is slaving away up there, white from exhaustion and plastering. I am worn to a frazzle cleaning up the dust and filth and shoving furniture about. But Treasure somehow cannot bring herself to help us. She seems to have the vapours. She reads *Just 17* forever and drapes herself around the dog.

'Do something,' I snap. 'Sort out these drawers. Throw out some rubbish.' My sympathy for her predicament is on the wane. Her demolished bunk beds are piled in a million bits blocking the landing. 'You can move these down to the basement.'

'You've just told me to do this,' screeches Treasure,

scrabbling about in the drawers. Maddened by my torrent of orders she bursts from the spare room tearing at her hair. 'What do you want me to do first? Make your mind up.' It has slipped her mind that our home has been turned into this pit of hell for her sake.

The weeks pass by. As I feared, work, romance and family commitments regularly tear Lodger away from the decorating, prolonging our ordeal. Treasure and I approach insanity. Faced by a possible eternity in the dreaded spare room, she still will not sort out the Everest of plastic bags. I may not help her. She guards her possessions like a Rottweiler, snapping and snarling fiercely at my approach. I dare not enter. I continue with the hoovering, sweeping and furniture removals.

Egged on by Lodger, Treasure is eager to discard all her existing furniture. Gleaming new shelving from floor to ceiling is now a must, regardless of expense. Lodger whirls Treasure off in the car to buy it. He is shocked by my parsimony and convinced that were he constructing the dog's bedroom, no expense would be spared. Lodger and I bicker like anything. We are a pack of Rottweilers.

Then suddenly it is finished. Lodger and I are no longer speaking but Treasure has come to life. She is moving in and tidying, sorting, arranging, throwing away and whistling. She has found heaven. She phones Rosie with a glowing report. Only one thing mars her happiness. Me. I am allowed to admire her chamber from the doorway but barred from entering.

'Go away,' snaps Treasure. 'I know what I'm doing. Just leave me alone. And don't speak to my friends. No one wants to speak to you Mum.'

The mountain of bags has gone. Somewhere among   129

them were my earrings, best mascara, nail-clippers and favourite T-shirt, which Treasure has sneaked away over the years. I shall never find them now. They are hidden in the blue room.

The dog at table

Treasure is having a difficult week, what with romantic dramas and her room being decorated. For a special treat I rather childishly allow the dog to sit at the table and have a tiny bit of apple pie and ice-cream – its absolute favourite. We have moved a large garden chair into the kitchen which fits the dog to perfection.

Treasure is cheered by this little event. The dog manages rather well, we think, for its first time and without any hands. We all have our pie together. No doubt our behaviour will be frowned upon, mine particularly as ringleader.

'Lodger will go mad,' says Treasure, ever so pleased. He is frequently distressed by our lack of hygiene regarding the dog. Were he to have spotted us all at table he would never have permitted himself to eat there again. I disinfect the table and scrub it thoroughly.

Lodger appears the next morning looking rather grumpy in his spotless white towelling dressing gown.

'There's an enormous pile of sick in the kitchen,' says he looking shocked. 'I've covered it with newspaper. Was

131

it your pie?' He smirks. He has taken this opportunity to denigrate my cooking once more. He has guessed half the truth but luckily knows nothing of last night's anthropomorphism.

Recently Lodger has grown increasingly concerned over the general standard of hygiene in our home. He has begun to refuse all offers of food, fearing that it may be contaminated with dog. Somehow during its preparation I may have touched the dog and then a cooking utensil or ingredient.

There was a time when we all ate happily together, but now Lodger's fears have ruined everything. He refuses my offer of delicious spinach quiche and ostentatiously sends out for a pizza. But who knows what the pizza chef may have been up to? Grandma is always wary of strange male cooks. She has no proof that they ever wash their hands.

The telephone:
Part 3

For weeks now I have been squabbling with British Telecom, querying my last squillion-pound bill. They have replied politely, finally sending me a special twenty-five-page itemised list of every single call made within a three-week period. I am shocked to the core. It accuses Treasure and me of making almost five hundred calls in three weeks. This puts our average at about twenty-four calls a day. Does even Treasure have the time or number of acquaintances to make this possible?

I cannot believe the list. Shaking with fury I sit down for hours and hours, ticking off the calls to each number. Gradually the truth emerges. A forest of ticks appears around each of Treasure's friends' numbers, Rosie's having the most ticks. How is the Treasure managing it? Outgoing calls are barred and I am watching her like a hawk.

Studying my data I find that Treasure is possibly doing cluster calling. 'Please may I call Rosie?' she will say, polite as anything. Charmed, I remove the secret barring code. Treasure then rushes to the upstairs phone and in

133

the twinkling of an eye, presumably rings several friends in rapid succession, pretending to have rung only one. The sly creature plays the telephone like a keyboard. She doesn't poke amateurishly at the numbers with one finger, but dials in a flash, her practised fingers dancing over the digits at the speed of light. She can thus call the next chum without a perceptible break in the conversation.

This cluster calling is a good wheeze. I cannot catch her out unless I stand at her elbow on the alert for the end of a call, then wham in the secret code before she does another one. But this would be invasion of privacy. I cannot monitor even the Treasure to this degree.

I hold up the tell-tale sheet of calculations. 'Look,' I scream, pointing at the tick forests. 'Look at this. These are YOUR FRIENDS' NUMBERS.'

'I'm sorry,' says Treasure. 'I won't do it any more.' For a few seconds she looks slightly nervous, almost contrite. There is her mother, source of all pocket money, in a dreadful and justified temper. Treasure quickly recovers herself. 'What else can I do?' asks she, remembering that attack is the best means of defence. 'I've said I'm sorry.'

'Pay for it.' Treasure leaves the room a martyr. She thought an apology would be adequate.

My advisers are horrified. 'This is theft,' says Mrs B. 'She is taking your property without your permission.' Mrs B is possibly right. One could see it that way. Treasure has taken the best part of £200. My call barring has been ineffective. I have not applied it ruthlessly enough.

I try harder. For days I guard the telephone ferociously. Treasure is allowed only four outgoing calls per day. She becomes the scourge of the neighbours, begging them desperately for the use of their telephones. It still seems to be against her principles to use the phone box round the corner.

Soon she becomes restless and agitated. Without unlimited access to the telephone she cannot remain calmly in the house for more than a few minutes. She repeatedly darts out on her bicycle, summoning Tom the perfect boy to accompany her on these wild forays. I had not, until now, appreciated the sedative effect of the telephone. But still I bar it. To harden my heart I mull over a few pages of the itemised list.

I introduce new regulations. Every phone call is to be written down. Between us Treasure and I achieve a new average of six to ten calls a day. But for how long can we sustain this regime? By the third week it is crumbling. I catch Treasure making a small cluster call. I can spot them if the person she initially rang is not the person she says goodbye to. We are living in a climate of tension and suspicion.

And then I receive another piece of advice. I must regard the telephoning as a part of Treasure's social life. She is socialising without roaming the streets and clubs. I should be thankful. It may cost an arm and a leg but a least Treasure is safe at home. And the socialising can be done in small chunks, under my supervision, and interspersed with homework and practice.

But Treasure is not alone in her affliction. Rosie apparently socialises in the same way. She rings later in the evening for the third time.

'Please can I speak to Treasure?'

'What did you want her for now?'

'Nothing much,' says Rosie dreamily. 'I just haven't spoken to her for an hour.'

Treasure and the generation gap

I am driving Treasure and Rosie to Brighton. The plan is that if Treasure has a chum with her, Brighton will be more fun and she won't have to slop around sulking at her grandparents' and great auntie's.

She and Rosie select some particularly vile music to play on the way down in the car. They can't sing the tunes, there aren't any, but they chant, shout and repeat bits in a jolly way. I am worried that the dog may go deaf in the back with its ears next to the speakers.

'E's good, E's good, E's good,' raps Treasure. This little phrase makes the girls laugh like anything. They rock about the car, shouting out the odd repeated word. Somehow the relentless monotony of the music eludes them. It modulates nowhere. I can barely detect even a change of chord.

'What's this music called?' I ask prissily.

'Oh blanks,' says Treasure, 'you're so sad Mum.' She and Rosie are weak with laughter. I cannot understand Treasure's vocabulary. Blanks is a new one, so is Egg. Treasure's translations are rather garbled. This must be the generation gap, which I thought I had trendily avoided. I long for Fats Domino.

I am allowed one side of the Fats tape. Treasure herself bought it for me for Christmas. I put it on my list and since then, somewhere along the line of peers, this tape has been approved, as have the Rolling Stones. I may listen to them in public as long as I don't sing snatches of tune. Treasure doesn't seem to mind that her mother is an elderly ex-rocker, provided that I behave with absolute decorum and do not move a muscle while listening.

She caught my friend and me watching videos of *Ready Steady Go* rather soppily the other day. It brought back our youth. Oblivious of Treasure's opinions, he tapped his feet, hummed tunes and jiggled about. There we were – both sixteen again. Treasure sneered horribly the next day. 'He's weird,' said she rolling her eyes. 'Your friend's weird. What's the matter with him?'

Fortunately Grandma and Grandpa have no suitable audio equipment, only a primitive gramophone in the corner. But anyway Treasure and Rosie gollop down their enormous roast dinner and are off in a trice to the pier. Grandma is off to play bridge and Grandpa, recently out of hospital, closely resembling a walking corpse and still hiccupping, demands to be driven to the car salesroom and to the betting shop – his lifeline. He absolutely must visit it daily. He totters to the counter and back, po-faced, the amount of his winnings a closely guarded secret. He is in a grump.

'If I hadn't been in hospital last week I'd have won the *whole* car,' he snaps. 'Don't tell Grandma.' Gasping for breath he directs me to the car showroom. He shuffles towards the salesman, yellow with exhaustion.

'I'm not dead,' he croaks. 'I still want my car.' I drive Grandpa home. He rests immediately. I take the dog to visit Auntie. She is waiting to feed it Hovis, buttered and neatly cut into squares. The dog is now Auntie's surrogate great niece as Treasure has become rather stingy with her visits of late.

I return to the grandparents. Grandpa lies comatose on the sofa.

'They're back.' He points feebly towards the bedroom.

Treasure and Rosie are putting on one roller boot each and preparing for a skate. It is five fifteen, the train leaves at six, but they must have a skate first. They are to travel back alone, a thrilling prospect, proceed to the Strobe and stay the night at Rosie's house while I remain down in Hove in the elders' compound. The generation gap has turned into a chasm. The grandparents and I watch *Casualty* together. It is lovely and quiet without Treasure but rather strange. We cannot decide whether we like it or not.

Terrifying
shopping

Treasure got a Wonderbra in the end, but before she'd had time to wear it more than half a dozen times it was too small. So she says. I am not allowed to look. Perhaps it is no longer à la mode. So today we go to collect a rather more demure one, already ordered and waiting to be picked up.

The lady in Selby's cannot find it for the life of her. Treasure and I begin to feel rather grumpy. We set out on these expeditions in an enthusiastic way but fate seems to be against us. Anyway this time we decide not to be cast down. Leaving the brassiere lady emptying her cupboard for the second time, we nip over to Top Shop.

Things are going swimmingly. Treasure and I perk up and find some frocks and bikinis. All we need now is to try them on. We hit another obstacle. All two changing cubicles are full up. For ever. Treasure eventually gets into a minuscule one but I continue to wait. Time passes, a queue forms, people start going red in the face. Still the lady in the large cubicle fiddles about, wondering and wondering about the length of her new trousers.

She comes in and out to ask her boyfriend's opinion rather frequently. At last she vacates the cubicle. I rather unwisely criticise her as she does so.

'Thank God for that,' say I crabbily, but I have picked a termagant. Just beyond the flimsy cubicle curtains I can hear her rampaging about roaring abuse.

'That cow,' she bellows. 'She is winding me up SERIOUSLY.' She rants on. 'And her daughter, trying on bikinis. What do they want? The whole bloody shop?'

Treasure appears by my curtain trembling. Her embarrassing mother has once again asked for trouble and she has been dragged into the fight. She is worried that the wild woman with the new trousers will be out there by the till waiting to give me a bop on the nose. 'She's still out there,' whispers Treasure, clinging to the curtain.

Luckily the coast is clear by the time we emerge. We are safe but shaken. And then up comes the brassiere lady waving triumphantly. She has found the brassiere. A thrilling outing all round. United by adversity and a common enemy, Treasure and I quite forget to bicker. Invigorated by the peril in Selby's we go on a wild spending spree. This brush with violence seems to have made me reckless. After the brassiere, frocks and bikinis, we buy hair glints, rugs, shoes and felafels. Even Treasure is staggered by my extravagance.

'Do you think we'd better not spend any more money?' she asks. Sometimes we exchange roles and it is Treasure's turn to curb my behaviour.

Treasure the supervisor

My long-term romance of several years has turned to ashes. Treasure and Rosie find me snivelling quietly at the kitchen table.

'Never mind Mum,' says Treasure. 'He was too fat anyway.' This is an essential criterion to Treasure. She and Rosie run to the corner shop and bring me back a lovely bunch of flowers. Treasure is ever so sympathetic, perhaps because she never considered him up to scratch anyway. They would snipe away at each other.

'Hallo Twit-Face,' said he.

'Hallo Stupid,' replied Treasure. Which one was the fourteen-year-old? Treasure was probably right. My relationship with him was deeply flawed. I should have known it from the moment he declared his love of Andrew Lloyd Webber musicals, but I carried on, blindly.

Treasure objected wildly to my dates with him. She considered my behaviour utterly depraved. 'You are a prostitute,' she roared. 'You are the only mother in the whole school who stays out so late. I am ashamed. I'm

141

going to speak to Miss Harold (headmistress) about you. Go away,' she shrieked. 'Don't speak to me about this. I hate you. I woke up at one o'clock, I wanted a drink and you WEREN'T THERE. You only care about HIM.'

Grandma holds the opposite view. 'You must go out and enjoy yourself,' she commands, dead keen for me to find a partner. Grandma believes that a chap will protect me from murderers, robbers, conmen and the workhouse. She is keen to see me set up with such a person before she leaves this world. Alone I am an incompetent in many ways and in permanent danger.

I am Grandma's baby and Treasure's mummy. I may not stay in and I may not go out. Grandma is desperate for me to find lasting romance, Treasure is not. She is continually on the alert for any sign of a new one. All phone calls and visitors are closely monitored.

Treasure enters my room as I speak to a male acquaintance on the telephone. She begins to smirk at once. She suspects a new romance. It is her duty to stamp it out immediately. She sits on the end of the bed spluttering and repeating my remarks in a loud whisper.

'Robert,' she whispers. 'Ooooh.' She rolls about the bed. 'Who's Robert?' She is an eight-stone wasp, dangerous when antagonised. I cannot swat her away – a scuffle will ensue and my conversation, spoilt anyway, will be terminally ruined. I give up and put the phone down.

'You're blushing.' Treasure rolls about pointing at me in a mocking way and clutching her stomach. Tears roll down her cheeks. She is helpless, in pain laughing. For

142

some reason I cannot get my face into the appropriate shape and give her the drubbing she deserves. I find myself laughing nervously. Treasure assumes that she has amused me.

'You've got a boyfriend, you've got a boyfriend,' she carries on in a noxious sing-song. She is eight years old again. Her suspicions aroused by the phone call, she interrogates me further.

'Are you going out tonight?' she asks. 'Please go out.' She wants me out of the way before her friends arrive, but only on certain conditions.

'Yes.'

'Where are you going?'

'To the theatre with Alison.'

'Some social life.' Treasure is unimpressed. 'Really thrilling.' She bounces from the kitchen, secure in the knowledge that no chaps are involved. But she is most displeased with my next outing. Who am I going with? I tell her.

'You're not to go out with him.' Treasure stamps and roars about the kitchen. 'How dare you? You're not to do that. He's a friend of Rosie's mother's friend. How embarrassing. You're NOT GOING.'

I reassure Treasure that this is a business dinner. She is slightly mollified. 'What time are you coming home?' She glares suspiciously.

'Twelve o'clock.'

'Oh yes?' she sneers. 'I bet.' Vile memories of HIM have reared up. She perhaps expects that another silly and provoking visitor will be round. For whole evenings I will not be in attendance. The telephone will be bunged up by my twittering phone calls. Treasure is keen to sabotage things before they reach this intolerable stage again.

It is difficult for me to conduct an adult relationship under these conditions. I find that I am suddenly thrilled by the thought of reading *Peter Rabbit* in Latin. Dead languages are perhaps easier than live relationships.

An almost pleasant morning for us

It is difficult to get Treasure out of bed in the mornings.

'Time to get up.' I try my best to sound agreeable.

'Leave me alone,' groans the Treasure. I am a prison guard suggesting a cold shower followed by porridge, not her mummy with a glass of orange juice.

'Just ten minutes,' begs Treasure. 'Just go away.' Our first fight of the day usually begins here. But today is different. Treasure wakes up independently. She enters my bedroom speaking in a civil manner. She wishes to get dressed immediately, she asks politely for breakfast and eats it all up.

Outside the almond blossom is pink in the sunshine. 'I love the summer,' says Treasure. Our morning is heaven. Carried away, I offer Treasure a lift to school. I am able to do this on the way to the Heath with the dog. We are easily in time for school but for some reason the dog is loth to enter the car. It crawls in and creeps about looking sick.

'Get her out,' screeches Treasure. 'She's going to be sick.'

I let the dog out. It staggers up and down the pavement retching. It is ruining our morning. Treasure is fortunately still in a merry mood, amused by its strange bandy walk. I rush it back into the house. It throws up on the hall carpet. I hurry back to the car, still just in time for school. Off we go.

We choose the same radio station, and drive along chatting. Such happiness cannot last. It doesn't. Half way down the Camden Road I change gear, inadvertently snagging Treasure's black tights on my ring. An immediate hole forms, an enormous ladder runs down to her toes.

'Why did you do that?' screams Treasure. 'You've ruined my whole day. Everyone will take the piss.' With a wild stab at the button, Treasure ejects my compilation tape. A snatch of Classic FM breaks through and enrages her further.

'You can turn the tights round.' I am trying to remain calm.

'Don't be so stupid. I hate you. These are my absolute best tights.'

'Who pays for them?' I enquire bitterly. I feel that perhaps a malevolent deity has it in for us.

'Are you going to give me some money?' Treasure is issuing an order, not making a polite request. We snap away at each other.

'Try saying please.'

'You never said sorry.'

Treasure and I often have short bursts of happiness like this which end in sudden tragedy. It seems difficult for Treasure to sustain a pleasant mood for long while the spectre of her mother lurks close at hand. In my presence she is very sensitive to small accidents. They

146

upset her deeply – laddered tights, a stale biscuit, rain, a broken remote control, a bruised knee. If I am nearby, I have caused them on purpose. Treasure is rather more resilient in the presence of peers.

I return home to clean up the dog sick. I notice that the almond blossom is in fact almost dead in places.

Treasure's high standards

The chic new décor in Treasure's room seems to have gone to her head. She now demands a very high standard of hygiene, generosity, etiquette and modesty at all times. I must be constantly on my guard, especially when Treasure's friends are visiting.

Leaving my bath emptying, I rush up to my room to answer the telephone and collect my clothes. To the best of my knowledge Treasure and Rosie are still asleep. Minutes later Treasure calls, hoarse with panic. 'Quickly, quickly, come here. The bath. Do the bath.'

She is in a blue funk. Rosie has woken up and is about to enter the bathroom, where she will spot the grime and disorder that I have sluttishly left behind.

I rush down towards the bathroom to complete the tidying. I am wearing my new underwear from Fenwicks. Treasure is horrified.

'NO. Stop. Go back. You can't come down like that.' Behind her Rosie is emerging from the bedroom. 'Mother. Please.' Treasure shields her friend from the offensive sight.

148

'But you wanted the bathroom cleaned,' say I, coyly hiding on the landing. 'I'm sure Rosie's seen her own mother.'

'Rosie's mother doesn't look like a bloody porn queen,' roars Treasure at top volume, giving up her attempt at manners.

'Look away Rosie,' I say, trying to make light of this event. Treasure's description is, after all, grossly inaccurate. I scurry into the bathroom and clean the bath scrupulously. I shout out a warning before reappearing, modestly covered in towels.

I can do nothing right. My every move brings on a fit. In public and in private Treasure is permanently on the alert for my bad conduct. She is particularly strict in the car. I tap my fingers on the driving wheel. 'Stop it,' she screeches. 'Will you just stop that.'

I try to distract her. 'Mrs Perez's famous relative lives along here,' I say, keeping an eye on the houses.

'Will you please watch the road,' roars Treasure. 'You're frightening me.' I stare obediently ahead. I spot the house.

'There it is! The green one.'

Treasure shrieks with horror. 'Stop it, stop it. You gave me a shock. Stop shouting. Just drive properly.'

At the sight of the grandparents' new three piece suite Treasure hits rock bottom. It is better than ours. 'Why didn't you get one like this?' she snaps petulantly. 'Ours is horrid.' She lies on the sofa for hours looking glum. Grandma is thrilled. She bought the whole lot for £100 from her friend, who bought it from Harrods.

My faults are mounting up. I am vulgar, irritating, tasteless and, worst of all, mean. Treasure spots this 149 final character defect in the sweet shop in Hove as we buy Great Auntie an Easter egg. There is one penny change. Thoughtlessly I take it. I turn round to see Treasure standing aghast at the shop doorway. She stares at me as if at a ghoul. What can have horrified her so?

'How can you be so disgusting?' Treasure spits out each syllable. She is rigid with loathing. 'How could you do that? Go and give it back.'

'Give what back?'

'You know perfectly well.' Treasure hisses contemptuously. Once out in the street she is free to shout. 'That penny. How could you take ONE PENNY? Are you EVER going to get yourself together?' She stamps off to Great Auntie's flat. Only one afternoon to go down here by the seaside before we are off home again and Treasure will be able to hide away in the pristine heaven of her new room. Without her mother.

Treasure's bicycle

Treasure is desperate for a bicycle. She is always desperate for the next thing that she wants. Without it she cannot imagine a tolerable future.

I am not keen for her to have a bicycle. Whizzing along the inner-city red routes, she may soon have no future at all. I imagine her mangled beneath a lorry in the Holloway Road. But I have rashly promised her a bicycle for months. Too weedy to say no, I used delaying tactics. Birthday and Christmas were too cold, I said, wait till spring. I can now trump up no more excuses. And why should she suddenly not have a bicycle? She has always had bicycles – smaller ones. But this one is a mountain bike, too large to go on the pavement. And her friend Darren has lent her an ace crash helmet. She sees herself winging over the Heath in the sunshine.

'You're not allowed to ride bicycles on the Heath,' say I sulkily. The dog has almost been struck down by meteoric and illegal cyclists.

Treasure is horrified by my treachery. 'You promised,' she whimpers. 'You can't change your mind.'

She is pale with shock. Remembering the squillion-pound phone bill I say I can't afford it. I am playing my last card.

'You'll have to pay for it yourself.'

'How much?'

'Half.'

Treasure has to sit down. She never imagined she had such a callous mother. But it is cowardice that drives me on. I have droned on to advisers that I don't want Treasure to have a bike. I now dare not tell them that I have given in. They saw no problem. 'Just tell her she can't have one,' they said sternly. 'It's your decision. There need be no discussion.'

But there was discussion. Hours and hours of heart-rending pleading, begging, arguing, screaming and weeping. I give in. Mrs Perez is horrified at my capitulation.

'I don't want to talk about this,' says she crossly, stamping from the house. 'Don't speak to me about it. You are hopeless.' She goes off in a bate without finishing her lemon tea.

Treasure and I go to the bicycle shop. There is the irresistible bicycle. It is in a sale, a once in a lifetime bargain. It must be purchased NOW. This fits perfectly with Treasure's penchant for instant gratification. She will not realise that nowadays sales last forever.

We buy it. Treasure can scarcely bear to listen to the bicycle man's instructions on how to work the padlock. She is overcome with ennui. If there is one thing she cannot stand, it is a calm and patient explanation. Everything must be thrilling and instantly comprehensible. As he bends over the bicycle explaining away, Treasure gazes dreamily around the shop. She wishes to

152

be out on the bike this second and whizzing along the street.

We escape. Treasure zooms off on her bike. I go home in the car. She arrives back forty minutes later with a screeching of brakes and in a dreadful temper. She was forced to return to the shop, have the brakes checked and listen to another explanation.

'I had to take it back three times,' she gabbles, demented with boredom. 'It still doesn't work. Listen.' She twirls about the street, brakes screeching. 'See.' Probably the bicycle man had explained that new brakes often squeak, but she wouldn't have absorbed this information.

'You'll have to take it back again.'

'No.' Treasure grits her teeth. She looks resigned. Fate has chosen her as one who must suffer.

The bicycle is now stuck in the hall tripping people up and spoiling the décor. Treasure hasn't used it much for the last fortnight. Perhaps because the weather has been inclement. And she can't work the padlock.

Passing the dog test

The dog has a soft, squashed, black velvety face. Treasure and I are forever squeezing it. It has a particularly droopy way of sitting that makes it irresistible to us. We are making everyone sick. Grandma is very irritated by this squeezing of the dog's chops. She is nervous of germs. We try not to do it in her presence. She can, however, see the attraction.

Lodger cannot. His disgust is peaking and threatens to ruin the harmony of our home. He now refuses to touch any tea-towels, fearing that our tainted hands may have touched them, or the dog may have breathed on them. He has taken to using kitchen roll to wipe up – a rather extravagant alternative. Lodger must be desperate. But I find that hostility from Lodger or anyone else only intensifies my desire to squeeze the dog. And it is a saintly animal. Even Mrs Perez has grown fond of it, despite its vicious squabbles with her cat, which has now sadly passed away.

Perhaps Lodger is under stress. He has announced that he plans to leave and set up home with his beloved.

The acquisition of a large new mortgage rarely lifts the spirits. And I must admit that the dog's manners are sometimes pretty grim. Only the other day I knelt down to adjust the video and it jumped up on my back in a rather disgusting way in front of a visitor. I fought it off as quickly as possible, but I had been hoping that evening to seem sophisticated. Will I ever see the visitor again?

Visitors have to be rather robust if they are to continue visiting what with the dog's overt displays of affection and Treasure's displays of hostility and loud background noise. Many have fallen by the wayside. Perhaps they could regard it as a sort of indoor Duke of Edinburgh's award scheme, for strengthening character.

Luckily Treasure rather liked the visitor who witnessed the dog's revolting behaviour. 'I like X,' said she. 'I don't mind him coming round. You can marry him if you want.'

This is the first time that Treasure has seen X. Perhaps he'd better not be told of her plans for his future. He might feel that they are rather precipitous.

The comparative behaviour of boys

My friend Mrs H tells me that her son, until recently an absolutely flawless boy, has suddenly begun to play up. He doesn't screech or cling to telephones, but is a brooding, critical presence in the house. He has recently managed a bit of bonding with his father, from which my friend is, of course, excluded. This makes her even more of an outcast in her own home.

She had a little drink at a neighbouring party and stumbled slightly in the kitchen, laughed, righted herself, but there was the boy, looking daggers.

'You're drunk,' he hissed. 'How disgusting. Go home at once.'

She wasn't drunk at all. The more she smiled cheerily to reassure him, the more repulsed he was. He strode off in a temper. Meanwhile at home he refuses to take off his school uniform on any account. It's a very hot black blazer that he wears and he will sit muffled up in it, sweating and brandishing his dirty fingernails at table. Girls have started ringing up and spots are emerging. Perhaps this is why he won't go out.

He is the third boy I've heard of who won't go out. They stay in, read books and diddle with computers. One plays chess.

Mrs H brought the boy and his sister out to dinner with some grown-ups. I went to the dinner alone. I had invited the Treasure, but she considered it a rather pitiful offer. She preferred to stay in and play with the telephone. Sitting opposite Mrs H's children I sensed the critical presence. Both children wore black and maintained almost complete silence. The boy sat tense and pale with revulsion. We all chattered away. Some grown-ups made the rather foolish mistake of trying to chum up with the boy and his sister.

He spoke cruelly of these fools as Mrs H drove him home in the car.

'How pathetic,' said he, in a terrifyingly adult tone. 'You could see that all those people hated one another. You haven't done anyone any favours getting *them* all together.' Mrs H felt rather crushed. 'And the worst one was that Helen,' he continued relentlessly. 'The tragic thing was that she thought everyone liked her, and nobody did. It was quite obvious.'

Mrs H often has to endure this contemptuous treatment. Treasure's critiques are almost loving by comparison. I mentioned this boy's downfall to Treasure. He is an acquaintance of hers.

'So?' says she.

'But he won't take his uniform off.'

'Why should he?' Treasure looks puzzled. I list the other complaints.

'But he's fourteen,' explains Treasure. 'What's the matter with you?' She gives me a half-amused and

157

withering smile. My friend and I are pitiful creatures.

A few days later Mrs H rings again. Luckily a saviour has turned up – next door's hamster, while next door are on holiday. 'It's brought out a tenderness in him,' says she soppily. She has even heard him saying 'Kootchy-koo' and other things like that. Naturally the hamster likes the blazer. It scuttles up the sleeves, bravely approaching the armpit, where it is forced to turn back. Mrs H also has a pond full of newts, which her husband likes to go out and stare at. He is forever doing it. The fellows in her house are obviously deeply affected by animals.

Another friend rings with news of her son. He is so far from perfect that in despair they have visited the therapist together. The boy spoke interminably of the problems of adolescence. A little bored after several years of such griping my friend, to keep herself awake, started counting his favourite words. She counted twenty-two 'bollocks' in ten minutes. She felt I might like to know this. I did. It rather puts Treasure's bad language into the shade. She is Fairy Tinkerbell in comparison.

Bargain
or blackmail ?

Treasure has been invited to the party of a lifetime —
black tie, finishing at midnight, crammed with pop
stars and glitterati. Lizzie's daddy, a media person, has
invited the gang. I cannot refuse her request to go, even
on a school night. I do feel, however, that I can insist on
a few measly conditions: that she goes to bed early and
behaves pleasantly until party time. No screaming,
tantrumming, offensive language or heavy telephoning.
This should be within her capabilities. She has only two
evenings to go. I am not erecting impossible obstacles to
her happiness.

Treasure lasts one hour. Time is whizzing by and she
will not do her homework. 'I will do it when I want to,'
she shouts. 'I am trying to RELAX.'

This could escalate into party banning easy as pie. I
remain calm. 'Just watch it,' I say icily, 'if you want to go
to this party.'

Treasure contains herself. Just. Too late I realise
that my conditions were obviously a wild gamble. The
evening continues. Multiple phone calls pour in and out.

I ban them until the homework is finished. The bedtime deadline is fast approaching. Treasure is still relaxing. She tries on her party outfit and all my jewellery. She selects the best necklace and earrings. They go perfectly with the black worm dress. But time is snapping at Treasure's heels.

Brring, brring – the poisonous telephone rings again. A friend of Treasure's. They have a huge row. Through the wall I hear rabid bickering. Treasure is picking up steam, becoming agitated, still dressed in the worm and high heels and only ten minutes to bedtime. Will she make it? Will the party have to be banned?

'Get off the phone,' I say. 'You have ten minutes left. Argue tomorrow.' I ask a few more times. Countdown is about to start. In the nick of time Treasure relinquishes the phone, but she is demented. I have cruelly stopped her in the middle of a traumatic discussion. She bursts into my room.

'You're blackmailing me,' she screams, violet with temper. 'You're being horrible to make me upset so I can't go. You're doing it on purpose because you're jealous.' Slam. Treasure hurls herself on to her bed dead on time, weeping loudly and bitterly. This is not quite the calm early bedtime I had hoped for.

I am in a cleft stick here. I cannot bear Treasure to miss the party but I cannot afford to be inconsistent. Inconsistency, say all advisers strictly, has been my biggest mistake. I must never make a threat that I cannot carry out, they drone, forecasting doom.

I won't be able to carry this one out. Treasure would be heartbroken. And a verbal warning is out of the question. Any chance remark by me can be a flashpoint.

I try a new strategy. I write a warning letter instead. If there's any chance of a shriek, warns the letter, will Treasure please remain in her room and avoid her mother.

Next morning I wake Treasure with an orange juice and the letter. It is a success. But it is a huge struggle for Treasure not to have the last word. If there is anything she must have, it is the last word. Were I to stand over her with an axe dripping blood, she would still have it. She is bold as brass. Nothing on earth will stop Treasure from answering back. She must do it, even now.

'I just want to say ONE THING,' says she, white-faced, fists clenched. 'Will you just let me say ONE THING?'

'Say it.'

'You were very mean to interrupt my phone call last night.'

'Very sorry,' I say and leave the room at top speed, otherwise I might want to answer back. I am also rather keen on having the last word. Our battles over it are continuous. This time Treasure may have it without a fight. I will set a shining example of self-control. And Treasure will go to the party.

Treasure goes to the party

On the eve of the party a sudden obstacle rears its head. Treasure does not have her ticket. An angel of mercy, I race to Lizzie's mother's house in the car to fetch it. My altruism is rewarded. I am offered a ticket for myself. But can I accept it? I feel that my presence at the party may cast a pall over the event for Treasure. Lizzie's mother is very encouraging. There are five hundred people going, says she. Treasure won't even see me.

I decide to go for an hour or two at the end, before bringing Treasure home. For some reason I think I might enjoy myself. I break the news carefully to Treasure.

'I've got a ticket too,' I tell her, 'but don't worry, I'm only coming for a bit at the end.'

'I don't mind,' says Treasure pleasantly. She is full of surprises. But all her chums are here and it is party time. The air is thick with squeals and spray perfume. Large girls fill the bathroom, bedrooms and staircases. They are all on the move, from one mirror and wardrobe to another. Between showering and shrieking and trying

162

on and making-up, they need the odd sandwich. I am in demand. Treasure has once again stolen my eyeliner.

Everyone is tremendously glamorous. Robert arrives in a smart bow tie. Treasure's worm dress is fearfully clinging, but at least it is long. Rosie's is very short, Chloe's is shorter. 'If I bend over you can see my bum,' says Chloe. She is right. The slightest tilt exposes the bum. Fortunately there are some additional fringes which partially conceal it.

Suddenly Treasure decides it is time to go. At once. A scented chattering crowd fills the hall. Treasure is now wearing my mac. It hangs off her shoulders in a strange way. 'Robert says I look like a hooker in this mac,' says she.

'If you feel like a hooker perhaps I could have my mac back.'

'No you can't.' Robert has borrowed Treasure's blazer. His own is too small. Will we ever see hers again? Off we go. Everyone totters to the car. The mandatory pop music is turned on during the drive and conversation is rather risqué.

'I'm going to pull a politician,' says Chloe. Shrieks.

'And I'm having an old man to be my sugar daddy,' says Rosie. Much more shrieking.

'And I'm having XX,' says Treasure, bagsying a pop star.

I drop this cluster of brazen creatures outside the party, but dare not leave them out on the streets of Bloomsbury in this condition. I plan to lurk in the car on guard until they are safely inside. Treasure spots me.

'Go away Mum. Will you just GO AWAY.' Out of sight I kerb crawl until they are indoors, and then drive home to the lovely silent house.

163

Returning later for my hour of party I notice that although this is a grown-ups' event, it is more suitable for youth. There is Treasure up by the stage with her friends, bopping around. Apart from the girls the dance floor is almost deserted. A bunch of helium balloons floats in the middle and two oddly dressed adult show-offs dance alone.

I spot Rosie's mother. I scream hallo over the million decibel music. We both lip-read for a moment. Treasure bounces up. This is her kind of heaven. She has met stars and DJs, she has drunk wine, she has arranged and eaten free snacks. She still needs yet more entertainment. 'Please can I stay the night at Rosie's? Please please?'

'No.' She rushes back for another bop near the stage. Most guests are speaking in sign language around the edges of the dance floor, or out in the bar and lobby. Probably only the hardened guests remain. The weak have gone home deafened hours ago. I have a shout at a few more people I recognise. Treasure bounces about, backwards and forwards, here for a hug and a shout, back for a bop. I feel rather elderly. I am desperate to be home again. There is nothing like a modern dance floor to send me whizzing home to the dog and my cocoa.

Luckily it is nearly home time. There is much screeching on the pavement as Treasure and her friends say emotional goodbyes. A crosspatch usher tries unsuccessfully to silence them. Treasure staggers happily towards the car. She suddenly realises she is crippled and removes the giant high heels, but it has been worth it.

Treasure's footwear

I hear a loud clumping and stumbling sound on the stairs outside my bedroom. Treasure is wearing her clogs. She often has difficulties with this footwear. Only last week she fell off a bus, seriously injuring her knee and ripping her new, astronomically priced second-hand jeans. She seemed rather elated by this accident.

'Guess what?' says she, ever so excited. 'I just fell off a bus. I was just waiting to get off and this person pushed past me and I lost my balance.' Treasure seems to feel that this is something of an achievement. The clogs are a source of adventure. She continues to stagger about in them whenever she possibly can.

They are an enormous impediment while shopping. 'Don't go so fast,' hisses Treasure, trying not to move her lips. 'I'm wearing my clogs.' We crawl along the High Street. Treasure has of necessity developed a special clog walk – a fusion of clomp and glide. The result is rather stately. She swans along the pavement in a rather majestic way, several inches taller than usual, sometimes leaving in her wake a trail of gaping men.

165

'Whooaarrr!' went a couple of them. I find this rather worrying. I have suggested some lovely flat Clarks' sandals, but Treasure is disgusted at the thought. She must wear huge clomping heels. All shoes must be clog-like and black. Even sandals must be raised upon giant wodge heels. Potential ankle-crackers.

Back in the seventies, my friend Mrs H had a serious accident in her clogs. She fell down a stone staircase in a stylish house in Italy. But then, she remembers, the clogs had a purpose – to provide a plinth for the bell-bottoms, which otherwise dragged in the filth. But today's bell-bottoms are shorter, says she. The clogs are no longer essential. Only in Holland, for flat surfaces or clopping along the top of a dyke, perhaps.

But Treasure will not be parted from hers. She must wear them daily. Tonight she is going to the Strobe in the new clogs. They are hopeless for bopping. She has already sworn never to wear clogs there again after closely escaping death by trampling last time. It is fatal to fall off the clogs in the Strobe crush.

'I thought you weren't wearing clogs there again?'

'I'm not going *into* the Strobe,' says Treasure wearily. 'I'm going to the station.'

'What for?'

'We've got to meet someone,' says Treasure in a cagey way. 'We've got to be there by nine thirty.' She and Rosie clomp off into the drizzle.

They are now keen on hanging out by the station. Four corners of this hideous junction seem to attract them: the Strobe corner, the station corner, the fish and chip shop corner and the corner sporting a mini-market, where Treasure once worked as an underpaid and exploited child labourer. Youth clusters on these corners, sitting on steps, standing about in a suspicious way. Treasure has grown tremendously fond of this junction. She attempts to flit from corner to corner while the traffic zooms past from five different directions, through three sets of traffic lights, drunks stagger past from the pub, the odd psychopath is probably lurking in a darkened doorway. Grandma saw it all on *Crimewatch* and rang at once to alert us.

Treasure can no longer run away briskly and escape these inner-city hazards. She will be wearing her clogs.

The saintly side of Treasure

Treasure's baby half-sister was born this week. We whizz to the hospital to see it. It is snoozing peacefully when we arrive but immediately begins to bellow. In its two whole days of life this has never happened before. Baby sister has a staggeringly loud voice. In rushes a midwife to help with the purple, rigid, shrieking baby. It is throwing itself about in a fury. 'Wind,' says the midwife. Its first attack, specially for us. Twenty minutes of intense screeching ensue.

Treasure behaves impeccably. She coos over Baby and holds it. She is the ideal hospital visitor. The mummy and I compare and contrast births. Treasure arrived in a tearing hurry and slept for most of the next ten months. She was a perfect baby. She looks perfect now, sitting on the bed drinking her tea politely.

We go down to the canteen for a snack. Once safely alone with her mother Treasure begins to snarl. She issues a scathing reprimand in the lift. 'You are SO embarrassing,' says she. 'That was disgusting the way you talked about contractions. You are SO disgusting.'

Weak with shame Treasure demands an enormous meal in the canteen. It soothes her a little. We return to the birth unit for more cooing at Baby.

Treasure has always behaved in a saintly way towards relatives and friends in hospital or in dire emergencies. She will sit for hours at a bedside, keeping a sharp lookout for any signs of impatience on my part. At the first twitch she will give me a stare of extreme severity.

Grandma has fond memories of Treasure's devotion and attentiveness in the past.

'Grandma is very poorly,' said I. 'We are going to see her first thing in the morning.'

'We must go NOW,' commanded Treasure, packing her bags in a frenzy. She didn't realise that the thought of us driving at night throws Grandma into a cold, sweating terror, and this state of anxiety may exacerbate the angina. But Treasure was persistent. We went immediately, without telling Grandma of our perilous voyage, and arriving by surprise. Treasure moved into the nursing home for whole days, chatting away, attending to Grandma's every need. She took charge. Grandma was entranced. I supplied transport and food to complement the appalling nursing home diet. Grandma is not accustomed to a sausage roll and half a cup of tinned soup served at 5 p.m. as the last meal of the day. Salads had to be brought in and other essential dietary supplements. Grandpa had to be supervised at home. Grandma is convinced that when alone he will set fire to the toaster. Treasure and I formed a team.

Treasure has also sat at Great Auntie's bedside for an eternity while I drove around looking for all-night chemists and emergency prescriptions. She has helped to repeatedly haul a delirious Grandpa back into bed and stay for hours with a blind, elderly neighbour. Since her nursing home experience, Grandma has always been perplexed by the versatility of Treasure's personality.

Now here is Treasure just longing to babysit the new sister. She is keen to do more hospital visiting. She has her photo taken holding Baby. She is in heaven.

Normal snarling, grump mode is resumed in the car on the way home. Treasure needs more skin-coloured tights to go with the dreaded summer school skirt.

'Can't you wear white socks?'

Treasure can take no more. 'I've told you already. I am a SENIOR. I'm not talking about this any more. Don't speak to me.'

Another tense and silent drive follows. The hospital charm has vanished without trace. I am rather piqued that I receive so little of it.

Lodger's departure

Things are rather twitchy in our house. Lodger is soon to leave and set up a new home with his beloved. He and I have never really chummed up again since he frittered half my savings on the glamorous new shelving in Treasure's room.

He has, however, done his best to be pleasant since our squabble. As I have been rather crabby of late, Lodger purchased from passing traders a dustbinful of horse manure to cheer me up. I arrive home to find it blocking the front path.

'What's this for?' I ask waspishly.

'I thought you might want it,' says Lodger, looking considerate. Could there be a subtext here? I have never received a tub full of excrement for a present before. And it isn't even a present. It was just a favour. Lodger thought I would be desolate if I missed the manure men, so he stepped in on my behalf.

'Don't you want it?' asks he gently.

'Not really.' I suggest rather unpleasantly that he perhaps keep it in his rooms. Worse has been deposited

171

there in the past. In the dog's youth it once scrambled all the way up to Lodger's chambers on the top floor and made rather a nasty mess. One could have thought that a large cow had been wandering across the carpet. When Lodger returned home he unwittingly trod in what the dog had left behind and trampled it all about – up and down the stairs, into his living room. Naturally he was wild with fury.

But why should the dog have gone all the way upstairs to relieve itself when it was obviously in a hurry? It spurned the newspaper on the stone kitchen floor (which it usually used when caught short) and must have dashed up to Lodger's carpet like greased lightning.

After a short discussion, Treasure and I concluded that the dog was making a statement. This was its only way of expressing its resentment at Lodger's behaviour: hiding its biscuits and football, taunting it with snacks and even throwing it into the air. Apart from his wild extravagance regarding the decorating, Lodger's treatment of the dog has been his gravest misdemeanour. It has almost resulted in his dismissal. However, my reprimands combined with The Statement seem to have cured him.

Fortunately the dog does have many other admirers. Young men are keen to take her for walks. Her huge muscles, ferocious expression, foaming slabber, rampant sexuality regardless of gender and fondness for football rather endear her to them. They are not ashamed to be seen about with such a butch dog. They wouldn't take a poodle.

172   And today I see a bunch of purple carnations on

the kitchen table. 'They're for you,' says Lodger charmingly. Perhaps I am being harsh. We have had some pleasant times. And the Treasure has grown rather fond of him.

Treasure's school uniform

I have bought Treasure her school summer skirt, a vital part of her uniform, as we seem to be having a bit of a summer. Last year the sun hid until late July, giving Treasure little opportunity to wear the skirt. Then she lost it rather promptly. This is the second such garment. It is inoffensive and luckily replaces the summer frock, in which no person on earth could look chic.

But like the last skirt, this one is too long. Treasure will not contemplate wearing it in its present condition, just below the knee. Naturally she wants it hoisted up to just below the bum. Headmistress will not be pleased.

I turn it up. In case Headmistress orders it turned down again I refuse to cut a chunk off. This makes the hem rather lumpy. I fiddle about for hours pinning and sewing away. Then I iron it nicely. To my mind, this is a most hateful way of spending an evening. I hope Treasure will be grateful.

She is not. The next morning she rejects her skirt out of hand. It is not short enough. She also objects wildly to the fat hem, even though it is almost imperceptible after my flawless ironing.

What I would very much like to do is to stand over her with a large whip and insist that she unpick and resew the miles of hem again herself, working into the early hours like I did, blinded and maddened by the thousand weeny stitches and magically self-tangling cotton. I would like her to realise what her rejection means.

'I'm not bloody doing it again,' I shout coarsely. 'You can wear it like this or do without.'

Treasure stamps off in her winter skirt. Nothing on earth will force her to wear an unattractive garment. I have made my usual big mistake – an unenforceable threat. Treasure will stick to the winter skirt. No amount of threats or deprivations will sway her, and my money and effort will be wasted.

In a fury I rip out my million little stitches and hack off yards of unwanted skirt. I hem it to bum length. Not only have I spent two evenings stabbing away at the sewing, but I am about to be inconsistent again. Treasure has won hands down. While I prod away at the blinding green and white stripes I glance up now and again at *Riders* on the telly. Buttocks, crops and zips flash by. It is another evening of torture.

In the morning I give Treasure the skimpy result. The jade is satisfied. She prances off to school in it wearing black tights. She comes home in a rage. The black tights are not allowed. Only skin colour. This is unfortunate. Black tights added a rather demure look to the ensemble. Skin-coloured emphasise the brevity of the skirt. They are also rather chilly.

175

'I'm so cold,' moans Treasure in the morning, stamping off in her flimsy outfit. Summer seems to be over. We have now had two solid days of aggravation over the uniform, but strangely enough, Treasure is secretly fond of it. She had always longed for one and to look like a 'proper schoolgirl'. And it freed her from the daily nightmare decision of what to wear. And now here is an extra surprise bonus. She can rail non-stop against its strictures.

Watching television

Treasure's persistent television watching is beginning to grate on Grandma's nerves when we visit Hove. It is the way in which Treasure sits stultified before it that depresses Grandma. She has obviously been hoping for a chat with Treasure, but she is out of luck. The alluring television has Treasure in its thrall and she, debilitated by the rigours of life in town, is too weak to resist. She uses Hove and her grandparents' flat as a convalescent home. She lies, fondling the dog's chops and watching the television and the hours pass by, bringing the grandparents no pleasure.

Television in our house, however, is something of a mixed blessing. It calms and pacifies the Treasure and so brings periods of tranquillity into our lives. It is her opiate. Unfortunately these periods can be rather extensive. They extend particularly when homework looms or bedtime approaches. They plunge Treasure into a torpor from which nothing can extract her except the magical ring of the telephone.

Any other form of interruption – a little question

from me, the distant sound of the hoover, a reminder that dinner is on the table – will evoke a furious response, rather like prodding a snoozing hornet.

It is risky even to sit next to Treasure on the sofa while she is watching. For some reason she must sit on the left side of the sofa, and any slight infringement of her space, any joggling or movement, or even a sigh, will drive her wild with temper. It goes without saying that any attempt to change channels, once Treasure has made her choice, will cause uproar.

She does have difficulty making her choice, due to a confusing set of priorities. Sometimes, although watching a gripping serial, Treasure will flick channels to check on the adverts on the other side, and there are some adverts with which she is enraptured. She will miss the serial to which she has been glued, during which no one may breathe, whisper or move, in order to admire the favourite advert.

Fortunately all these horrors are avoidable. Treasure now has a television in her room to which she may retreat or be banished. This alternative television can isolate the Treasure and render her catatonic. Meanwhile, down-stairs, I can watch any programme I like, phone my friends and entertain visitors without interruption, have secret snacks and lie along the whole sofa. Compared to the telephone, this is happiness at a knock-down price.

Sometimes, on better days, Treasure and I eat our dinner before the television. This means no rows at table and less criticism of the menu. But there are risks involved when watching television together. Treasure will ask multitudinous questions about the programme. Today she spots Marilyn Monroe's coffin.

'When did she die?' asks Treasure. 'Was she murdered? Why? How old was she? Why did President Kennedy have girlfriends? How many? How do you know?' Treasure's questioning is never finite. It leads all over the place and wrecks the rest of the programme. This often rather spoils our television dinners, and it illustrates to a tee Treasure's double standards. No one may ask *her* a single question while she is watching television.

Grandma unwisely ignores this edict when Treasure is viewing in Hove. She will ask loud questions regardless.

'Do you want pie?' roars Grandma. 'What do you want on it? Yoghurt or vanilla ice-cream?'

'Anything,' snaps the Treasure rudely. She is being offered an exquisite home-made pastry, but who would know it?

Grandma will not accept such a vague answer. She continues to bellow. 'Make your bloody mind up.' Grandma wins. She is a tornado blowing around the television. Treasure knows she must answer or lose sight of her programme in the storm.

'Yoghurt.' She answers as briskly as possible using minimum words. 'Please' would be superfluous.

School rules

Treasure has received another drubbing from Headmistress. The hated summer skirt is too short. Headmistress has ordered that it be taken down to its original shop length. Treasure is in a fury. Furthermore, Headmistress has instructed that Treasure unpick it herself. She must now slave away to turn herself into a drudge. No wonder she is feeling rebellious.

'Everyone else's is exactly the same,' rages Treasure. 'We all measured. Me, Sally, Carol, Hazel and Chloe.'

'Perhaps your legs are longer and the skirt looks shorter.'

Treasure stamps with temper. 'No. We measured from the knee up. She just picks on me. It's not fair.'

Treasure has clashed with Headmistress before when she dyed her hair orange in parts. It was intended to be subtly golden but certain fair areas turned a rather bold shade. Treasure sailed into school like a beacon and was instantly reprimanded. I was spoken to by Headmistress. 'If we allow this,' said she, smiling in a charming way, 'then the next thing we know people will be dyeing their hair green.'

'Absolutely,' said I, siding with the enemy, because I am secretly thrilled that school is enforcing rigid boundaries like mad: neat hair, sensible shoes, long skirts, silence in class and no swearing. I feel this is the perfect antidote to the laxity in our home, where outrageous clothing, foul language and fairly monstrous behaviour are the norm.

Treasure and I tried all sorts of remedies for the hair – repeated washing, soaking in coconut oil, followed by wrapping in polythene and towels, but the beacon only faded slightly. Fortunately Headmistress relented, impressed by our efforts at obedience. The beacon faded gradually. But this time Treasure is being rather brazen. She flounces off to school the next day without having lengthened her skirt. She is always one to push her luck.

And the skirt isn't the only problem. Treasure has lost a huge tract of homework and is wearing plimsolls instead of her proper school shoes. The clog-induced blisters on her feet make any other footwear unbearable. And large callouses have sprouted on her heels, possibly due to the modish way in which she leaves her laces undone, making the shoes rub up and down on her heels causing havoc.

I ring Headmistress to explain the skirt, the limping and the lost homework. She is in a pleasant mood, unlike the termagant that Treasure had described. She even offered, she said, to take the hem down herself. She has perhaps not yet noticed that Treasure has taken to wearing bicycle shorts under her skirt. Treasure seems to treat the skirt as a decorative frill rather than a modest item of clothing.

This weekend she must sew and adjust the skirt

181

herself. This is a fearsome prospect. Treasure has never had a sewing lesson.

'What?' shouts an adviser. 'Fourteen and can't sew?'

'They don't teach sewing any more.' I explain. 'They have CDT instead.'

'Then you teach her.'

'I can't teach her anything,' say I, remembering the violin practice and the French homework and the algebra.

'For God's sake,' screams my adviser, 'just ENABLE her to do it. Give her a needle and cotton, show her a few stitches and let her get on with it. You can do that, can't you?'

No. I have to admit I can't. It may seem simple from the outside but the adviser has forgotten the legion things that could go wrong: thread refusing to go through the needle, tangling cotton, annoying knots, pricked fingers. Any one of these could drive Treasure into a fury in a trice, and they will be MY fault. And then there's the time it will take. Treasure might manage a five-minute sew but she would never survive the yards of hem.

Perhaps this is something else I could leave school to deal with. I remind Treasure that Headmistress kindly offered to do the hem herself.

'That's right,' hisses Treasure. 'She said she'd rip it down on the spot.'

Whoever am I to believe?

Our outing

Treasure meets me at a small drinks party in a perilous area of King's Cross. She arrives with dramatic news. Her friend Chloe has behaved abominably. Treasure travelled miles across London to visit and wasn't even offered a snack. They have fallen out terminally.

'I'm SO ANNOYED,' announces Treasure, bouncing in. She heads for the wine and peanuts. She feels that this trauma entitles her to a drink.

'Just a little taste,' I say.

'It's alright,' says Treasure confidently. 'Children are allowed to drink as much as they want with meals. The peanuts are the meal.' She guzzles wine and peanuts and reviles the friend. This is a private view. Treasure studies the pictures in a sophisticated way. Then she meets a contemporary. She is able to tell her horrifying story again. She seems none the worse for her wine.

I am. One glass has had a devastating effect. I feel rather resentful about this. I am unable to drink like other adults. One glass, whatever quality, gives me a murderous headache. I feel it looming half-way through the glass. I dare not touch a second. Treasure and I stagger arm in arm to a nearby Italian restaurant. She is thrilled that we are going out to dinner together in what she feels to be a state of inebriation.

We enter the restaurant in a good mood. The staff conspire at once to make it a bad one. The waitress is new and charming but doesn't speak English. She smiles attractively but cannot understand our order. We point to it in both languages repeatedly. Unpleasant background music has been turned on and the restaurant is almost empty. Since my last visit, standards here seem to have fallen significantly. What has happened? Time creeps by. Treasure starts to twitch. I send her to phone Rosie, hoping that a chat will help her to endure the interminable wait for food.

Fifty minutes later Waitress returns smiling still and with the wrong order for me. Treasure shares her prawns, swimming in butter. The mixture of wine and adversity seems to have turned her into a saint. Even the next course cannot dampen her spirits. She has ordered roast chicken with peppers. Concealed beneath a huge mound of peppers and drowning in a pool of oil lies one square millimetre of chicken. Treasure isn't keen on peppers. It was the chicken she was longing for. Still she hardly complains. 'Never mind,' says she. 'You can have the peppers.'

I have unwisely ordered squid. It too is swimming in grease. I eat Treasure's peppers. As this outing is meant to be a treat, Treasure and I go home in a taxi. I feel rather sick in the taxi. I have a crippling stomach ache. I apparently cannot eat or drink to the slightest excess without immediate retribution from somewhere. But despite the oceans of grease, abysmal service, pain and discomfort, we rather liked our outing. In fact it has been a roaring success. Treasure wants to do it again.

'We haven't done anything like this for ages,' says she. We must obviously do it again. The success goes to my head. In a relaxed way I am lying down in the taxi, stretching my legs out in an effort to relieve my excruciating stomach ache. I am letting standards slide. But Treasure realises that they must be maintained. There can be no let up.

'Sit up properly Mummy,' says she strictly.

'I can't. I feel very sick.'

'You can't be sick,' says Treasure, shocked to the marrow. 'You're a mother.'

The several ages of Treasure

Treasure's age is variable. It varies from three to thirty. She is sixteen to thirty while shopping, three to five getting ready for school and when poorly, ten to fifteen for homework and five to eighteen when visiting relatives. It is sometimes difficult to adjust to these sudden transformations.

Today we have an eleven to thirty shopping expedition. Treasure and I are going to buy Grandma's birthday present. This is a difficult task. Grandma is not particularly gracious when receiving presents.

'What did you waste your money for?' she will shout. 'I told you not to waste money. And don't buy me any flowers.'

We always defy her. We can tell if the present is a success by the degree of rudeness with which Grandma accepts it. She was most offensive about last year's blouse. Most of all she likes home-made items. They are free and show dedication and effort. This time we are to take an enormous risk by buying something unusual.

We drive to the market. We park. But as we leave the

car Treasure bumps into two friends on their way to Oxford Street. Can she go? Yes. We can buy Grandma's present tomorrow. I leave Treasure with her chums. I can now go home and work in absolute silence all afternoon.

I arrive home. Brring brrring. The dread telephone. 'Will you accept a call from a London payphone?'

It is Treasure, distraught. She has no change. She has changed her mind. She didn't want to go off with her friends, She is aged eleven. She wanted to stay with her mummy and go shopping. She feels terrible. She feels she has let me down. Too late she ran back round the corner, just in time to see me driving away. She roamed the one-way system looking for the car, but I had gone. She is in despair and alone. She wants to be with her mummy. Am I cross?

No. I drive back again. Fortunately she is only five minutes down the road. Treasure and I begin shopping in the market. She is fifteen and this is her idea of heaven. It is full of earrings, T-shirts, jossticks and felafels. This is not quite Grandma's style. And then Treasure spots the perfect present. A hat. A wide-brimmed panama with navy edging, just right for Grandma to wear in the sun on the promenade. I try it on. It is too large. I try another beige one. The beige one looks better. I can wear it if Grandma rejects it.

'Don't say that,' shouts Treasure bossily. 'You always say that. The other one is better. It's more Grandma. The beige one's too trendy.' She is right. She is now twenty-one. We buy the untrendy hat. Will Grandma like it? It's a toss-up.

But even I am growing to like the market. Treasure

and I sit by the canal in the sun eating vegetarian snacks and carrot cake. This is a pleasant interlude. We are both our correct age. Treasure has been right on two counts – she chose the better hat and the right person to go shopping with. Her mummy. This was an unexpected choice. I am usually an embarrassing impediment rather than an essential requirement. Treasure affects not to need her mummy much at present. Just on the odd occasion, depending on her age.

We are at Hove for Grandma's birthday. She is thrilled with her hat. By chance she is going to a wedding next week and a hat is just what she wanted. She has a little trouble with the brim tickling her neck, but the hat is a success. So is the first half-hour of our visit to Hove. Treasure eats her lunch up enthusiastically at table.

But there is a limit to the number of virtuous things that Treasure can do and this seems to be it. She has found and chosen the hat, eaten lunch properly and has now had enough of her mother and grandparents. She is seventeen and wishes to be alone. She needs to watch *Home and Away* in silence and then go out. 'I'm going to work on the beach,' says she rather aesthetically.

She returns four hours later just as Grandma and I are about to send out a search party, her feet covered in gigantic raw blisters. She has walked to Brighton Pier and back twice, partly in the dreaded clogs and partly barefoot in a romantic way along the beach with the tide out. We are now graced with her presence for the rest of the evening, but she is exhausted and functions only minimally. She can barely eat or speak – the two things that Grandma and Grandpa long most for her to do.

188 And we have another pressing engagement. We must

visit Great Auntie round the corner. Treasure may as well slump on Auntie's sofa as on Grandma's. She walks to Auntie's in bare feet because of the crippling blisters, and carrying her clogs. Why carry them?

'Because it looks as if I've just taken them off.'

Treasure flops on to Auntie's sofa. She is aged seven again. She keeps the hood of her jacket up and sucks her thumb. Luckily the dog eats up its squares of bread and jam and gives Auntie a big kiss. Auntie converses with me and the dog. She tries the Treasure. A few little words squeeze out, but Treasure cannot manage many. She is busy regressing on the sofa and her mouth is full of thumb.

Auntie and I give up and watch TV. Cowboys, Indians and a glamorous lady doctor are all sweating through a cholera epidemic. Luckily this is Auntie's favourite programme. Sometimes, in the past, she and I have left the television off, but Treasure still remained scarcely animated. Naturally Auntie is a little disappointed by this visit. She looks forward to Treasure's visits as if to the sun coming up, and then she gets an almost total eclipse. Every time.

On the way home I reprimand Treasure and accuse her of making nil effort. She is affronted.

'Yes I did,' she shouts. 'I was very nice to Auntie and she was very nice to me. You were the one who was horrid.'

This is a strange interpretation of events. Unless Treasure is eight again.

Holiday plans

Treasure and I begin to long for a continental holiday. Rather like childbirth, we have forgotten the discomfort of the last one and now want another. But can we afford it? I suggest camping in the South of France. Treasure is thrilled. My friend Mrs B is appalled. Am I mad? she asks. Don't I remember the debilitating heat, the mosquitoes, the boredom, and that I hate camping and healthy outdoor pursuits? And running across fields to shared lavatories? She forbids me to go. She shatters my dream. I had seen myself in a shady tent, typing away, while Treasure and Rosie were off swimming, discoing, windsurfing and flirting.

Mrs B looks rather sour. 'Oh very nice. You'll sit watching all that teenage fun while you're mouldering away growing more wrinkled by the minute. You'll hate it. You'll be bored. Who will you talk to? Forget it.' She is a pragmatist.

I forget it. Anyway, Treasure is planning more immediate and terrifying hols. She is keen to go to

Glastonbury. 'Rosie's going, Chloe's going, Lizzie's going. Rosie's mother's going. It's only £50.'

'Only if Rosie's mother's going.' The woman is a saint. Who else would brave the ghastly lavatories of a pop festival, the noise, the food queues, the drugs, the trampling, the mass sleeping outdoors, the inevitable rain?

I describe these hideous conditions – memories of my youth – to Treasure. 'We don't care,' she sings, dancing about the kitchen. 'We're teenagers. And Rosie's mother's going to stay in a hotel and we've got to meet her every day, and if we run out of money she'll give us food.'

More details of Treasure's holiday plans pour in daily. A huge tent is to be pitched in advance. Lizzie's father's tent. Lizzie knows how to work it. There's a cinema. Chloe's father's going. I could go. 'Why don't you come? You could stay in a hotel as well.'

I couldn't possibly. But I see that some sort of holiday is a must. I decide upon Cornwall. Why not? Other people go there and have a pleasant time. Sometimes the sun shines. It never has done on my visits but I am prepared to try again. Anyway, if I can find a resort with a disco, Treasure can live at night and sleep through the rainy days. And then there are Surfers Against Sewage, in whom Treasure has expressed an interest.

But this time I feel she must have a chum with her. Will we be able to find one who is available and whose parents will allow and can afford a holiday? Rosie's mother says yes. Hopefully Treasure and Rosie will not have a tempestuous row on the eve of our departure. Planning holidays is a dreadful gamble for us.

191

Ruder and ruder clothing

I sneaked off to the last designer clothes sale without Treasure. An adviser had ordered me to do it. She had, in the past, accompanied the two of us to one of these events and found it a harrowing experience. Treasure needed an attendant – to fetch more clothes in different sizes and colours, to consult on style, to admire her choices. She also had a dreadfully difficult time limiting her spending, which led to us squabbling in the mass changing area. Harassed by Treasure, I was unable to serenely choose new clothes or listen attentively to my adviser. It is difficult to feel relaxed and glamorous in a mass changing room, especially when in a vile temper, and so I went to the last sale alone.

Treasure was absolutely disgusted when she found out. 'How could you do that? You're so selfish and mean.' This time she spots the invitation coming through the letter box, pounces on it and hides it in her bedroom. She invites Rosie and her mother so there is no way I can sneak off again without her. We all go in a gang.

Treasure selects a rather daring mixture of garments:

one red satin top in the style of a corset, with matching skin-tight hot pants. The corset top is so tight it is splitting. Possibly other would-be vamps have also had a tough time getting into it. Fortunately Rosie's mum is present to point out this flaw. If I had pointed out the split Treasure would have thought it a plus. She rejects this ensemble.

She returns to the changing room with another selection of skin-tight garments. Fitting like a snake-skin, they need zips from top to bottom to allow the wearer entry. Treasure zips herself into the skirts and top. These horrors are even more erotic than the worm dress. They are rather revealing. The skirt zip goes from calf to waist. It is a feature as well as functional. The top neckline is most risqué, especially with the zip from neck to waist. Treasure doesn't care. She has fallen in love with these garments. The hussy *will* have them. I am nervous on two counts here: my shrinking bank balance and Treasure's safety when in public wearing slinky, zip-up snake outfits.

'Choose one,' I say meanly. 'A skirt or the top.'

Treasure looks crestfallen. She cannot make this heart-rending decision. She adores both garments.

'I'll pay,' she begs. 'I'll pay for one.'

'You still owe me some bicycle money.' I am heartless.

'Take it out of my bank,' says Treasure. 'I told you to take it.' She is pale with longing.

'Very well.' I speak in clipped tones. Treasure promises to go without pocket money until the clothes and the bicycle are paid off.

I am rather sullen on the drive home. I find it difficult to chatter gaily about Treasure's stunning new wardrobe. I, of course, have purchased nothing.

Hereditary anxiety

I go alone to visit the grandparents as Treasure's social calendar will not permit her to leave town. I meet a beggar on the tube on the way to Victoria. She is dressed in raggedy clothes and is accompanied by a small child. I shell out.

To keep the grandparents up to date I inform them, when I arrive in Hove, that the London Underground is now swarming with the homeless, rootless and indigent. Grandpa is unmoved. 'They have holidays in Majorca, those people,' says he knowledgeably. 'They make a fortune. You know that don't you?'

'I hope you didn't give her anything,' says Grandma, impressed by Grandpa's informative comments. They are both convinced that there are numerous occasions upon which I am likely to be taken for a sucker. Age and distance hamper Grandpa's efforts to save me. He tries. He sends cautionary features torn from his newspapers concerning hazards and charlatans of all sorts: rip-off insurance companies, the perils of night driving, car thieves, urban mugging, homes wrecked by teenage gatecrashers. He writes strict instructions in large capitals in the margin. 'NO PARTIES ALLOWED IN YOUR HOUSE,' accompanied recently by an anxious letter, 'Beware of thieves and rascals who will always be around you. Your loving Papa.'

From distant Hove the grandparents can only issue these dire warnings and worry. They are on permanent red alert. Their daughter and granddaughter live in a teeming stew of vice, corruption, criminal activity and exploding bombs. Our every move seems hazardous. This is more or less accurate, but we have to pretend that it isn't so that they can sometimes relax and sleep at night.

Only last week I met the Perez boy off a train at Victoria. Two bomb scares occurred during my ten-minute wait. The Perez boy and I escaped breathless and pale with shock. I made the rather foolish mistake of telling Grandma about this incident. She was enraged. Why had I risked my life to pick up someone else's child? I must promise never to do that again. And to lock the car doors from the inside while driving about and never to go out in the dark.

Their terror is heightened as Treasure grows older and more independent. 'Do not let that girl out of your sight,' roars Grandpa. 'Do you hear me?'

They would be totally opposed to the modern notion that a child must be allowed to take risks in order to learn to cope with danger. I have not mentioned it to them. But they are trying to loosen up. When in Hove Treasure is now allowed to walk five minutes round the corner to Great Auntie's flat in broad daylight on her own. As I am a grown-up I am allowed out with the dog at night, but I must carry Grandpa's shillelagh, a vicious, spiked blackthorn club with which I can fight off maniacs. Even Hove is dangerous.

I dare not tell them about Treasure's short walk in town. Off she went down the road last Sunday to collect her Dr Martens from Lizzie's house. It was late afternoon, the sun still shining. This was intended to be a low key outing. Treasure was aiming at a quiet day to try and retain some strength for school on Monday. She returned thirty minutes later with tales of horror. She had spotted a terrified elderly lady pursued by a raging drunk. Along came the police, sirens wailing, and chased the drunk away. Treasure collected her Dr Martens and on the way back encountered the elderly lady again, still petrified and begging for protection. The drunk was after her again. He lumbered up to Treasure and the quaking woman and started roaring at them.

'Look,' said Treasure strictly, 'what do you want?'

'Seven Sisters Road,' burbled the drunk.

'It's that way,' said Treasure fiercely, and off he went. Naturally she came home over-excited. The grandparents must never hear this story.

Even my travelling to Hove by train gives them the shudders. There is an enormous risk, they feel, that my bags will be stolen on the way back to town. Even if I escape marauders, I may still inadvertently leave a bag on the train – probably the one full of food supplies. Grandma writes my initials on it in capitals. I am still her baby. She now has two of us. I must ring the minute I arrive home, with all my luggage.

It is difficult to disregard the grandparents' anxiety. It is catching. I am worried to death about Treasure as she flits around with her friends at night. And now she

196

is planning her sojourn at Glastonbury again. I can think up all sorts of hair-raising scenarios. Vague memories of the pop festivals of my youth flash back to me – the rain, the discomfort, the crowds, the mess and the mile-long queue for the nightmare toilets. I see Treasure and her chums tramping over a muddy rain-soaked plain, through mounds of ragged punks and hippies, breathing the hash-filled air, pelted with Ecstasy tablets while the odd trip is secretly dropped into Treasure's Pepsi.

I describe a muted version of this hellish vision to Treasure.

'Don't be silly Mummy. You have to pay for a trip. No one gives them away.' She is losing patience. 'They don't put trips into drinks any more. No one can afford it.' She describes her camping plans in a reassuring way. 'Rosie and her dad are going down on Wednesday to pitch the tent. It's got three rooms and I need some new Dr Martens. I need them now so they won't be uncomfortable. When can we get them?' She is all practicality.

Treasure has everything highly organised. Lizzie's dad is driving the gang down in a van, Chloe's mum will be on site demanding a daily report and check-in. Today Treasure's gleaming multi-coloured ticket arrives. She is thrilled to bits. In her excitement she rashly tells Grandma about Glastonbury. The grandparents' imaginings are even wilder than mine. Grandma knows for certain that Treasure's tent will be invaded nightly by drug-crazed rapists. And if they don't get her, then influenza and exposure will. These are exactly my own thoughts. I pretend they are not.

'It's quite safe,' I tell Grandma. 'Lots of parents are going.' I sound confident as anything. But it won't do any good. The grandparents and I will be on the rack while Treasure is prancing around at Glastonbury.

I have consulted the advisers, of course. Safe as houses, they say. Nothing can happen with so many people around. No worse than the Strobe. I read the programme, attempting to face this problem head on. I notice a Healing Field, a Sacred Space and a 'quiet haven for Yoga and Tai Chi'. This does not sound quite the endroit for tearaways. Perhaps Treasure will be safe after all. I still expect a harrowing weekend. I shall fill it with gripping entertainments to keep the vile imaginings at bay. Along with inconsistency, I am told that irrational anxieties and over-protectiveness are my other big mistakes.

Treasure's timetable

Treasure is not all that fond of routine. Her timetable is subject to fancy – pasta for breakfast, bedtime in the afternoon, baths at lunchtime, dog walks at 10 p.m. The only rule she sticks to is one of immediacy. Once fancy dictates, it must be obeyed at once. That instant. Such spontaneity often clashes with my timetable.

Treasure is not always aware of my plans. How could she be? How is she to know that having done the hoovering, dog walking and shopping I am planning to begin a vital piece of written work? I lift my pen just as a fancy strikes Treasure.

'Mum,' she calls in an urgent tone. 'Will you please come and test my history?' She has just left the bath and is dressed in towels. This is the wrong outfit for history testing.

'I have just started this,' I say in a reasonable way.

'I've waited an hour,' snaps Treasure. 'Will you please come now?' It seems to her that I am deliberately sabotaging her progress. We often experience these clashes. The tap of a typewriter key or my voice on the telephone often reminds Treasure that her timetable requires my co-operation.

I am speaking to a sick friend on the telephone. Having mouldered at home for a week with the 'flu, he was hoping for a leisurely chat. Treasure's timetable won't allow it. Her friend is staying the night and needs attention at once.

'Lizzie has eczema,' says she, announcing a sudden and urgent disaster. 'She needs that ointment. Will you please come and find it?' Aware that I am speaking to a chap, Treasure realises that instant medical attention is vital. She stands glowering.

'Lizzie's eczema is really hurting,' says she, shocked to find that I will neglect a sick child in order to pander to a man. She gives me a rather scathing look. 'Don't bother,' says she snottily. 'Just carry on. That's right. Don't bother about Lizzie.'

I give up the phone call and rush to the sick bay. A minute area of Lizzie's eyelid is slightly red. I advise less eye make-up. I cannot find the ointment but it doesn't seem to matter. As I am now free to attend, I am no longer required. Treasure and Lizzie are going out.

I would like to discuss the weekend plans but Treasure cannot. She now hasn't the time. She doesn't know yet anyway. 'I've got to go now,' she snaps. 'I'm in a hurry.' Her timetable is very demanding and rather inflexible. It leaves her little time for speaking to her mother.

I often try to establish weekend plans in advance. Without prior knowledge of Treasure's timetable, it is difficult to plan my own. I ask Treasure for information.

200   'I don't know. Leave me alone, I'm busy.' Treasure

cannot spare a minute. She must watch *Neighbours* / phone Rosie / try on clothes / go across to Lizzie's house / ring Chloe back. She cannot possibly speak to me.

Sometimes I plan an outing blindly, as if I am free to whizz about town at will. It is bound to clash with Treasure's timetable. I often need to ring in from wherever I am, to keep up to the minute on Treasure's plans; where she's going, for how long, how will she get home from some God-forsaken hole, when will I collect her? My friends have begun to jeer and taunt. 'Just ringing to check,' they say in a mocking way. 'She's just góing to check again.' This has become a catch phrase.

It's easy for them to jeer. They have boys who rarely go out or speak or think of romance. They sit about the house looking sulky. Sometimes they even join the grown-ups for dinner, looking critical and limiting conversation. Perhaps they need a slightly heavier timetable.

Treasure and the feminine mystique

Treasure has a pale and delicate skin. If exposed to strong sun for more than a few minutes it will burn scarlet and Treasure will be in horrible pain for days. She now faces a dilemma as the summer approaches and with it the time for bare legs. Treasure's are white as chalk. She will not expose them in this condition and she can never risk a real sun tan.

So she and Rosie decide to tan their legs instantly in unison, beginning in the early evening with a telephone consultation, comparing brands of cream. Cream is applied at 8 p.m. Wildly excited, Treasure tans her whole body. By 10 p.m. she is in despair. Rosie has telephoned to say that her tan is appearing, but Treasure's skin remains ghostly pale.

'It's not working,' wails Treasure, staring at her legs. We discover that Treasure's tan takes five hours and Rosie's only takes three. Treasure's results will not show up until 1 a.m. She goes to bed glumly but awakes to golden legs, a slightly paler body and blotchy ankles. This is more or less a success. Treasure conceals her ankles with socks.

I tell Mrs B about the tanning as we walk the dog. She is outraged. 'I think it's tragic,' she roars across the Heath, alerting the public, 'to be dissatisfied with your body so early. Only fourteen and she's already altering it.'

Mrs B is further horrified by my reports of shaving. 'My God,' she shouts, stamping along the sunny path. 'It's natural to have hair under your armpits.' People stop and stare. They think they have spotted a feminist. Mrs B continues to shout, thrilling the observers. 'I've never worn make-up,' she yells. 'I think it's bloody ridiculous.'

Mrs B mentions later over coffee that on every single one of her visits to our home she has observed Treasure involved in some sort of beauty preparation or process of feminine mystique. Today Treasure has colour-rinsed her hair and appears in a stylish towelling turban, reinforcing Mrs B's views. This is a disappointment for her after fifty years of fighting for feminism.

Fortunately for Mrs B, her child is a boy. Had it been a girl, I suggest it might have rebelled against her example and turned into a staunch fluffy. What a good job that I didn't wear quite enough frocks in Treasure's youth. Had I done so and plastered myself with make-up and earrings and chic handbags, Treasure might even now be pale and hairy as anything and sporting a boilersuit and crew cut, rather like I did in my youth. Grandma would be suicidal. But despite Mrs B's ravings I cannot disapprove of Treasure's style.

I did try, years ago, to introduce train sets and a selection of toys lacking in gender bias, but Treasure made a dash for the Sindy and Barbie dolls and played with them relentlessly for years, encouraged by the girls next door. Our home was wall to wall Sindy houses.

203

She then, to a degree, followed the example of these creatures. She has always aimed at gleaming hair, a flawless complexion, an hour-glass figure and a vast, up to the minute wardrobe. She has never given a fig for train sets or Scrabble.

Grandma and Grandpa have always been thrilled to pieces by Treasure's inclinations. She has been the charming little girl that I was not. She and Grandma have often played dressing up together, in frocks, frills, jewels, make-up and curlers. You wouldn't have caught me doing that. I'd have been out in the shed with a penknife. No one would have dared to mention curls. So the Treasure has brought Grandma happiness. Both grandparents have gazed at Treasure enraptured, scarcely able to believe their luck. They have had an angel in their living room. Now that Treasure is older, the angel appears less frequently.

The grandparents are not Treasure's only admirers. 'You should try modelling,' says the hairdresser, among others, egging Treasure on. She is dead keen already. She is rather peeved that I am not busily organising a modelling career for her.

'Why don't you do something about it?' she snaps. 'Everyone says I could do it but YOU won't let me.'

I foresee doom. Treasure, intoxicated by fame and riches, will flutter from catwalk to catwalk, her brain devoid of knowledge. But remembering my discussion with Mrs B, I realise that should I express disapproval of Treasure's chosen *métier*, she will be spurred on like anything. She may model, I say, provided she does not miss one second of school. She may, if the opportunity arises, model in the holidays and at weekends.

I dare not mention the modelling career to Mrs B, nor Treasure's choice of literature. Treasure is totally committed to *Just 17*. A visiting friend of mine, idly leafing through a copy, came upon a feature on summer sex. He was horrified. 'Does your daughter read this?' he asked, riveted to the pages. It was enormously informative. Every single body part that could possibly participate in summer sex was explained in a forthright way, much as one might explain the workings of a sewing machine or globe artichoke.

Mrs B was wrong about the mystique. There is none left, feminine or otherwise. Every function of every bit of every organ has obviously been described to all and sundry. On and on drone Treasure's magazines about the usual favourites: orgasms, wet dreams, masturbation and oral sex. For some reason I find this rather distasteful. I ask Treasure and her friend Robert whether such extensive knowledge is absolutely necessary.

'Knowledge is power,' says Robert cheerily, sitting at the kitchen table. 'You wouldn't want us to be ignorant would you?' Both smirk.

I wonder if there are any other areas of knowledge that they would pursue so assiduously. When Mrs B went home *her* son demanded that she take him to the library. 'I want to get out some Kafka,' said he.

Naturally Mrs B was tremendously impressed. Perhaps she is right after all and moral standards in our house are rather lax. Her son is fearfully strict. He has enforced a rigid ban on the capitalist press. Mrs B tells me rather proudly that he absolutely forbade her to look at the *Sunday Telegraph*, which usefully contained the whole week's television programmes. A friend had

205

brought it into the house. (Mrs B is not allowed to purchase it herself.) It might have saved her buying a paper all week if only her son had been more liberal.

This makes me change my mind again. Perhaps our house, rife with sexism, freely invaded by the evils of modern culture, is better after all. This week I am planning to use a striking coloured rinse on my hair.

The cultured side of Treasure

Today Treasure and I share a few elevated moments of culture and harmony. We are playing violin and piano together. Treasure has toiled away at the violin for years and now, several thousand pounds and five violin teachers later, we are reaping the benefits. It has been worth it, I am thinking, as Treasure swans through some Schubert, her intonation spot on, her tone delightful. I feel I am accompanying her in a rather sensitive way.

'Play louder,' commands Treasure. She has not yet mastered the art of being civil to her accompanist.

I play louder.

'You're not playing loud enough.' Treasure looks pained. She sees me as a saboteur. 'You're just not playing as nicely as you usually do. What's the matter with you? Play louder.'

I bang hell out of the piano. 'Loud enough?' I shout.

'No,' screams Treasure. 'You're doing it on purpose.'

I have often told Treasure that chamber music is meant to be a shared pleasure and at the first hint of 207 abusive behaviour on her part I shall leave the room. I rise from the piano stool.

'Where are you going? I am not being rude.' Treasure speaks in a quiet and menacing way, rigid with repressed temper. She holds her bow like a chain saw. She grits her teeth. 'I want to play the Mozart,' says she, each syllable escaping separately.

'Alright.' It is difficult to play Mozart while seething with hatred. We give up. We usually do. Occasionally we manage fifteen minutes of pleasure, but any attempt at instruction by myself will bring on a tantrum and early demise to the duets. Loaded with musical qualifications I must sit calmly and silently while Treasure massacres the dotted crotchets.

It is timing that fouls up the works. Treasure will not count beats in my presence. She will not count anything. She will not count me in. She lunges into a tune and I must guess, with my back to her, when the lunge is coming and be there.

'You count,' roars Treasure. 'Count. ONE TWO.'

I must count her in but I must never count through tricky bits. Treasure likes to skim through these pretending they are alright. But now, as her skill increases, melodic minors and third position loom and tricky bits rear up all over the place. If forced to deal with them Treasure will seize up or have a bit of a scream and run for the safety of the sofa and telly. Our duets are becoming more hazardous.

Sometimes I try to play alone. I am weeping happily over a heart-rending bit of Chopin that I have just discovered when Treasure stamps in crossly. 'Can you *not* play that piece. It's horrid. Can we play my Schubert?'

There is nothing that gets her practising like me trying to play alone. Treasure will want to come in, the dog will want to go out, Lodger will start tantrumming over my unfinished washing-up and the neighbour will want to borrow milk. My place is obviously in the galley.

Sometimes I take off my pinny and creep out to listen when Treasure and her violin teacher are alone together. Divine sounds float through the keyhole, difficult bits are repeated and interspersed with laughs. It probably has been worth it. Perhaps in a couple of decades, when this phase is over and I am almost dead, Treasure and I will have whole musical evenings together, now and again.

Other fiction of interest from Virago

THE MAGIC TOYSHOP

Angela Carter

'Angela Carter has the eye of a trompe d'oeil painter, bringing quite ordinary objects and scenes to vivid, sensuous, disturbing life. This works marvellously in *The Magic Toyshop*' – *Evening Standard*

Melanie walks in the midnight garden wearing her mother's wedding dress; naked she climbs the apple tree in the black of the moon. Disaster swiftly follows, transporting Melanie from rural comfort to London, to the Magic Toyshop; to the red-haired, dancing Finn who kisses her in the ruins of the pleasure gardens; the gentle Francie, who plays curious night music; dumb Aunt Margaret and, brooding over all, the sour and dangerous Uncle Philip whose love is reserved only for his life-sized puppets . . .

Original, visionary, and winner of the 1967 John Llewellyn Rhys Prize, *The Magic Toyshop* was made into a major British film in 1987.

MY BRILLIANT CAREER

Miles Franklin

'Remarkable . . . a marvellous story' – *The Times*

In this famous Australian novel, first published in 1901, the irrepressible and enchanting Sybylla Melvyn, aged sixteen, tells the story of her life. It is the 1890s. Sybylla, trapped in drudgery on her parents' outback farm, loves the wild Australian bushland and its way of life, but hates the bitter constraints and physical burdens which will always be her lot as a mere woman. Sybylla longs for beauty – to read, to think, to sing – but most of all to do great things, to have a 'brilliant career' as a writer.

Suddenly her life is transformed. Whisked away to live on her grandmother's gracious property, 'Caddagat', Sybylla captivates the rich and handsome Harry Beecham. As their love story reaches its inevitable conclusion we watch Sybylla choose between her brilliant dreams and everything conventional life can offer . . .

THREE TIMES TABLE

Sara Maitland

Three women – Rachel, her daughter, and her daughter's daughter – share a house, but inhabit different worlds. Fifteen-year-old Maggie flies with her dragon over the rooftops of London to a secret world; Phoebe, her mother, who has carried the values of the sixties into the harsher world of the eighties, is caught up in a private dilemma and confronts difficult truths about love and honesty; Rachel, the grandmother, an eminent paleontologist, has to reconsider the theories she has fought for throughout her professional life. Sara Maitland's remarkable novel focuses on one strange and wakeful night in which Rachel, Phoebe and Maggie find themselves facing the illusions of their own pasts. This is a powerful, magical novel about the shaping of women's lives – their work, their friendships, their mothers and fathers, the extent of their freedom and the boundaries of their experience. Rich and deeply perceptive, *Three Times Table* re-examines familiar issues and gives them a very contemporary turn.

NOT THE SWISS FAMILY ROBINSON

Fiona Cooper

'Reality and fantasy blur engagingly in this lesbian coming-of-age novel set in small-town US and peopled with charismatic humbugs' – *Independent on Sunday*

Monica Robinson, raised in the 'middle of nowhere', discovers early on that the American Dream isn't what it's cracked up to be. Even Pop, who likes the odd tipple, and Mom, whose blistering tongue rules the roost, ain't her real parents. What's more, they're sure fixed on the notion that she get herself a beau. Monica has other plans.

An afterschool job at Sam's bar is the means to stash away a few dollars. Meanwhile, her desirable English teacher entices Monica with tales of scholarship and, apparently, much more. Consumed with yearning and terrified by the dismal prospect of smalltown life in What Cheer, Monica takes a plane east and to England . . .

Angst, unrequited love and all the jostlings of adolescence converge in this humorous, sassy novel, written with Fiona Cooper's characteristic verve.

NIGHT FISHING

An Urban Tale

'The gap between the liberal right-on parents and the rudderless adolescents is sketched with compassion and great skill' – *Time Out*

Night Fishing is about sons who go wrong, mothers who don't see trouble until it's too late and fathers who aren't there. At the heart of this moving and all-too-familiar terror is Jaimie, a sweet boy, 'beautiful with a radiance', who finds the ultimate sweetness in street drugs. His mother is Janice, a documentary filmmaker who thinks she has her finger on the pulse; his father, a rich and famous man who sees the world through his camera lens; his friends, the teenagers who roam the back streets of London and tell their mothers they're just going night fishing.

With compassion and wit, the author of *Albany Park* has written a pithy, hard-hitting urban tragedy – a story for our times.

OUR SPOONS CAME FROM WOOLWORTHS

Barbara Comyns

'Barbara Comyns' distinctive manner is very much in evidence . . . sharp and engaging'
– *Times Literary Supplement*

Sophia is twenty-one-years old, she carries a newt around in her pocket and marries – in haste – a young artist called Charles. Swept into bohemian London of the thirties, Sophia is ill-equipped to cope: poverty, babies (however much loved) – and her husband – conspire to torment her. Hoping to add some spice to her life, Sophia takes up with the dismal, ageing art critic, Peregrine and learns to repent her marriage – and affair – at leisure. Repentance brings an abrupt end to a life of unpaid bills, unsold pictures and unwashed crockery, plus the hope of joys in store: this novel has a very happy ending . . .

This, the second of eight wonderfully eccentric novels by Barbara Comyns, first published in 1950, takes a tragi-comic look at artistic life in London before the Second World War through the child-like eyes of the endearing, ebullient Sophia.